Jacob suspected the game had changed the instant Anna walked into that bar.

She was no longer a naive coed. She was a powerful businesswoman—confident, cool, in control. Formidable for her business pedigree, she came from one of the most successful entrepreneurial families in history. Other men in the bar had taken notice, too. Her beauty only upped the intimidation factor, with thick brown hair falling around her shoulders, a dancer's grace and posture, and lips that suggested sweetness and hinted of a storm.

Anna's lips had fallen on his once—a few scorching heartbeats still emblazoned in his memory. The way she pressed against him had resonated to his core. She'd been so eager to surrender her body, so ready to explore his. Turning her down, saying he'd betray his brotherly friendship with Adam if things went further, had been the upstanding thing to do.

He'd been raised as a gentleman and no gentleman made a move on his best friend's sister, however tempting she might be. Anna had been astoundingly tempting.

Did he want to meet with gorgeous Anna Langford? The prospect, although ill-advised, was intriguing.

Pregnant by the Rival CEO

KAREN BOOTH

First Published in Great Britain 2016
By Mills & Boon, an imprint of HarperCollins*Publishers*
1 London Bridge Street, London, SE1 9GF

Large Print edition 2016

© 2016 Karen Booth

ISBN: 978-0-263-06626-5

Our policy is to use papers that are natural, renewable
and recyclable products and made from wood grown
in sustainable forests. The logging and manufacturing
processes conform to the legal environmental regulations
of the country of origin.

Printed and bound in Great Britain
by CPI Antony Rowe, Chippenham, Wiltshire

Karen Booth is a Midwestern girl transplanted in the South, raised on '80s music, Judy Blume and the films of John Hughes. She loves to write big-city love stories. When she takes a break from the art of romance, she's teaching her kids about good music, honing her Southern cooking skills or sweet-talking her supersupportive husband into mixing up a cocktail. You can learn more about Karen at karenbooth.net.

In memory of Holly Gilliatt,
brilliant author and fabulous friend.
You taught me the importance of
embracing the good and the
sheer power of defying the bad.

One

"Strangle me? Isn't that a little harsh?" Anna Langford gaped at her friend and coworker, Holly Louis.

The pair stood in the luxe lobby of The Miami Palm Hotel, just outside the bar. Anna was preparing to see her bold business plan to fruition. If only Holly could find it in her heart to say something encouraging.

"I've only been in a few meetings with your brother, but he's going to hit the roof when he finds out you want to cut a deal with Jacob Lin."

Anna glanced back over her shoulder. The bar was humming with people, all fellow attendees of the two-day Execu-Tech conference. As Senior Director of Technology Acquisitions for LangTel, the telecom her father had started before she was born, Anna had the job of scouting out the next big thing. Her brother Adam, current LangTel CEO, had been crystal clear—he expected to be dazzled.

The company had been floundering in the months since their father's death, and Anna had a bead on a game-changing cellphone technology, only Adam didn't know it. She was fairly sure that LangTel's competitors hadn't figured it out either. Unfortunately, getting to the next big thing meant going through Jacob Lin, and he absolutely hated her brother. Adam, without a doubt, despised him right back.

"That's him, isn't it?" Holly asked in a whisper, nodding in Jacob's direction. "Damn. I've never seen him in person before. He's fifty times hotter than in pictures."

Tell me about it. Anna was well acquainted with Jacob Lin and his hotness. She'd been rebuffed by him and his hotness. Six years later and it still stung.

"Does he always have that aura?" Holly swirled her hand in the air. "The one that says he's genetically superior to every man within a fifty-mile radius?"

Anna didn't even need to look. "Yes, and he comes by it honestly. It's not an act."

"Wow." Holly patted Anna's shoulder. "Well, good luck. I'd say you'll need it."

"What?" Any confidence Anna had mustered was evaporating. "Do you really think it's going to be that bad?"

"You're a Langford. He hates your family. So, yes. I do think it's going to be that bad."

"Technically, I could order you to come with me. You're a member of my team."

Holly shook her head so fast it made her curly hair frizz. "My job description does not include suicide missions."

Another wave of doubt hit Anna, but she did her best to brush it off. She had to do this. If she was ever going to convince her brother that it was okay to step aside and allow her to take over as CEO, just as he'd promised her before their father died, she had to make tough decisions and dangerous moves.

Holly wasn't wrong, though. There was no telling how Jacob would react given his history with the Langford family. "I'm telling you right now, it's going to be great." Anna feigned conviction. "Jacob is a money guy and I can offer him a big pile of money. And once Adam sees how huge this could be for LangTel, he'll get past the personal stuff, too. It's business. Nothing else."

"So what's your plan to approach Mr. Hottie?"

"I'm going to ask the bartender to give him a note."

Holly squinted one eye as if she had a migraine. "Oh, because that won't seem weird?"

"I can't call him," Anna pled. "I don't have his cell number." The only number she had for Jacob was six years old, acquired during the week he spent with her family at Christmas, the year she fell for him, the year she'd kissed him. The year he'd told her "no." That old cell number was no longer his. She'd tried it, and no dice.

"You can't exactly go up to him and start talking either. You won't just get the rumor mill going, you'll set it on fire."

"No. I can't just walk up to him." However ridiculous it sounded, if ever there was an understatement, that was it. Everyone in the tech world was aware of the feud between Adam Langford and Jacob Lin. The backstabbing had been ruthless and very public.

"If anyone can make the impossible happen, it's you," Holly said. "Text me later and let me know what happened. Good luck."

"Thanks," Anna muttered. She straightened her blouse and strode into the room with her head held high, then sidled up to the only available seat at the bar. She discreetly took a piece of paper and pen from her purse. It was time to conjure her steeliest tendencies. No looking back now.

Jacob,
I'm sitting at the far end of the bar. I need to meet with you to discuss a business proposition. I thought it best not to approach you in the open considering the state of things between you and Adam. Text me if you're interested.
Anna

She added her cell phone number and signaled to the bartender. She leaned forward, hoping the men sitting on either side of her wouldn't hear. "I need you to give this to the gentleman seated in the corner. The tall one in the gray suit. Black hair." She skipped the part about his ridiculously square jaw and sublime five o'clock shadow. She also left out his superhuman sexiness and his perfect, tawny complexion, the product of his Taiwanese and American background.

The bartender raised an eyebrow, looking down at the note.

Give me a break. Anna slid a ten-dollar bill across the bar.

The bartender swiped the money away. "Sure thing."

"And a dirty martini when you get a chance. Three olives." Liquid courage would be right on time. She scratched her head, striving to remain inconspicuous while studying Jacob. He ran his hand through his hair when he took the note from the bartender. She caught a glimpse of his deep brown eyes. It wasn't hard to remember the way they lit up when he smiled, but she doubted her message would prompt such a response.

His forehead crinkled as he read. What was he thinking? That she was crazy? Now that he had personal wealth north of one billion, was incredibly accomplished in the field of venture capitalism, and at the top of his game, it seemed a little childish to have sent a note. And to think she'd once hoped it would end well when she kissed him.

Jacob shook his head and folded the paper. He tapped away at his phone. How had she forgotten how bewitching his hands were? Like the rest of him, they were big and manly. They seemed so…capable. Sadly, her bodily familiarity with his hands didn't go beyond one of them on the small of her back and the other on her shoulder when he'd delivered the stinger that had stuck with her for years. *I can't, Anna. My friendship with Adam means too much.*

It had taken buckets of self-analysis to get over him, and just being in the same room was bringing it all back—in a deluge, where there was no dodging a drop of water. With all of the serious business-related thoughts rolling in her head, her mind kept drifting to their past—every smile, laugh, and flirtatious look they'd ever shared still haunted her. Dammit. She'd been so sure she was beyond this.

Jacob tucked his phone inside his suit coat pocket and finished his drink.

The screen on Anna's phone lit up. Her pulse throbbed in her throat. What would he say? That he wanted nothing to do with her or her family? That she was lucky he didn't call her out in the crowded bar?

She swallowed hard and read the text.

Penthouse suite. 15 minutes.

Anna forgot how to breathe. The message was so like Jacob. Direct. To the point. Just intimidating enough to make her doubt herself even more. She wasn't put off by powerful men. She worked alongside them every day, could hold her own in any tense business situation. But those men didn't have the pull on her that Jacob had once had. Those men hadn't once held her heart in their hands, and she sure hadn't spent years pining for any of them, writing dozens of heartfelt letters that she would ultimately never send.

Jacob stood and bid a farewell to a man he'd been talking to. With the grace of a cat, he wound his way through the jam-packed bar, towering above nearly everyone at six-foot and several more inches, acknowledging the few who had the guts to greet the most formidable and successful technology venture capitalist quite possibly ever.

A shiver crawled along Anna's spine as he came closer. He brushed past her, not saying a word, leaving behind his heady scent—sandalwood and citrus. Fifteen minutes. She had to pull herself together and prepare to be alone with the one man she would've once done anything for.

Anna Langford. I'll be damned. Jacob pressed the button for the private elevator to his suite. He'd spent the last six years convinced that the entire Langford family despised him, a feeling he'd had no choice but to return. After the note from Anna, he didn't know what to think, which was unsettling. He always knew what to think.

Did he want to meet with gorgeous Anna Langford, youngest of the three Langford siblings, the woman stuck with an untrustworthy jerk for an older brother? The prospect, although ill-advised, was intriguing. He and Anna had once been friends. On one memorable night they'd been a little more. But did he want to speak to Anna Langford, a member of the Lang-Tel executive board? On that count, it depended on what she wanted to discuss.

His plan to engineer a takeover of LangTel wouldn't simply backfire if Anna discovered it—he'd be sunk. The War Chest, a secret high-roller investment group led by Jacob, had watched the decline of LangTel stock after the death of Anna and Adam's father, Roger. The company was vulnerable with Adam in charge—he didn't have the confidence of the board of directors the way his dad had. LangTel was ripe for the picking.

The War Chest's plan had been born over cards and too much bourbon one night in Madrid, at a retreat for key players. Jacob had put it out there—*What about LangTel? Could a company that large be taken over?* It would be a daunting challenge, requiring a massive money pool and meticulous planning, but this was precisely the kind of project the War Chest loved. Without risk came no reward. There was money to be made, and a lot of it, because a company that well established would eventually rebound. Carving out a slice of revenge against Adam by ousting him as CEO would merely be giving Adam exactly what he deserved.

Jacob rode the elevator upstairs. The game had changed the instant Anna walked into that bar. She was no longer a wide-eyed coed. She was a powerful businesswoman—confident, cool, in control. Other men in the bar had taken notice, too—she was formidable for her business pedigree, coming from one of the most successful entrepreneurial families in US history. Her beauty only upped the intimidation factor, with thick brown hair falling around her shoulders, a dancer's grace and posture, and lips that suggested sweetness and hinted of a storm.

Anna's lips had fallen on his once—a few

scorching heartbeats still emblazoned in his memory. The way she pressed against him had resonated to his core. She'd been so eager to surrender her body, so ready to explore his. Turning her down, saying he'd destroy his brotherly friendship with Adam if things went further, had been the upstanding thing to do.

He had no way of knowing that Adam would betray him months later by ending their business partnership, making millions from the sale of the company they'd started together and publicly bashing Jacob's contribution to the project. The words Adam had said could never be erased from Jacob's memory. *It's your fault you never asked for a partnership agreement.* And to think he'd trusted Adam…that had been his first mistake.

He keyed into his suite—quiet, sprawling luxury, echoing his private existence at home in New York. Outside of a maid or a cook or an assistant, there was never anyone waiting when he walked through the door at the end of the day, and that was how he preferred it. Most people were nothing but a disappointment—Exhibit A, Adam Langford.

A business proposition. What was Anna's angle? It'd be brave of her if it involved peace-making. The feud between himself and Adam only continued to get worse.

It seemed as if the more successful Jacob became, the more Adam said crude things about him at cocktail parties and in business magazines. *Jacob Lin doesn't have an entrepreneurial mind. He's good with money and nothing else.* Jacob had given into it, too. *Adam Langford will coast on his family name for as long as the world lets him.* It was impossible not to engage, but it had also occurred to Jacob after the last barbs were exchanged in the newspapers, that words were no way to go. Actions spoke louder. He'd no longer tell the world what he thought of Adam. He'd show them.

Jacob picked up the direct line to the twenty-four-hour concierge.

"Good evening, Mr. Lin. How may I assist you?"

"Yes. Can you please send up a bottle of wine?"

He flipped through the room service menu. "The Montrachet, Domaine Marquis de Laguiche?" He rattled off the French with no problem. Years of shuttling between boarding schools in Europe and Asia had left him fluent in four languages—French, English, Japanese and Mandarin, the language his father had grown up speaking in Taiwan.

"Yes, Mr. Lin. We have the 2012 vintage for fifteen-hundred dollars. I trust that is acceptable?"

"Of course. Send it up right away." *Life is too short for cheap wine.*

Actually, he and Anna had consumed more than their fair share of cheap wine during their marathon late-night talks at the Langford family home in Manhattan. That felt like a lifetime ago.

His friendship with Adam had meant the world then. They told each other everything, commiserated over growing up with powerful, yet emotionally reclusive, fathers. They bonded over career aspirations, came up with ideas effortlessly. Jacob had hit it off with Anna equally well, except that he'd only had a sliver of time with her—ten days during which they drank, played cards and joked, while attraction pinged back and forth between them. He'd thought about acting on it many times, but never did.

He'd been raised as a gentleman and no gentleman made a move on his best friend's sister, however tempting she might be. Anna had been supremely tempting. It physically hurt to say "no" to her when she'd kissed him and it wasn't only because she'd given him a mind-numbing erection. He'd sensed that night that he was turning down more than sex. It was difficult not to harbor regrets.

After room service delivered the wine, Jacob removed his suit coat and tie. He was essentially shedding his armor, but it would make things more informal. If the Langfords were aware that a takeover was in the mix and Adam had sent her to spy on him, this would make him seem less threatening. The War Chest investors had been careful, but some tracks were impossible to cover.

The suite doorbell rang. Jacob had given his personal assistant the night off, so he strode through the marble-floored foyer to answer it. When he opened the door, he couldn't help himself—he had to drink in the vision of Anna. A stolen glimpse of her in the hotel bar had nothing on her up close. Her sweet smell, her chest rising and falling with each breath, sent reverberations through his body for which he was ill prepared.

"May I come in?" she asked. "Or did you answer just so you could slam the door in my face?" The look in her eyes said that she was only half kidding. He had to give her credit. It couldn't have been easy to break the silence between himself and the Langfords.

"Only your brother deserves that treatment. Not you." Jacob stepped aside. He'd forgotten about the sultry nature of her voice, the way it made parts of him rumble and quake.

"I won't take up your time. I'm sure you're busy." She came to a halt in the foyer, folded her hands in front of her, playing the role of steely vixen all too well.

"Anna, it's eight o'clock at night. Even I don't schedule my day nonstop. The evening is yours.

Whatever you want." The more time he spent with her, the more sure he could be of her motives.

She straightened her fitted black suit jacket. The long lines of her trousers showed off her lithe frame. "You sure?"

"Please. Come in. Sit."

Anna made her way into the living area and perched on the edge of the sofa. Palm trees fluttered in the wind outside. Miami moonlight filtered through the tall windows. "I came to talk about Sunny Side."

Of the things Jacob thought Anna might come to discuss, he hadn't considered this. "I'm impressed. I thought I'd managed to keep my investment role at Sunny Side quiet. Very quiet. Silent, in fact." Exactly as he hoped he'd kept his LangTel investments. Was he losing his touch? Or was Anna that good?

"I read about them on a tech blog. It took some digging to figure out where their money was coming from, but I eventually decided it had to be you, although that was just a hunch. Thank you for confirming my suspicions." She smiled and cocked an eyebrow, showing the same satisfied smirk her brother sometimes brandished.

The times Jacob had wanted to knock that look off Adam's face was countless, but on Anna? Coming from her, delivered via her smoky brown eyes, it was almost too hot to bear. He was intrigued by this sly side of her, more self-assured than the coltish twenty-year-old he'd first met. "Well done. Would you like a glass of wine? I have a bottle on ice."

Anna hesitated. "It's probably best if we keep our conversation strictly business."

"There's no business between you and me without the personal creeping in. Your family and I are forever enmeshed." She could turn this point on him later if she learned of the War Chest's plans, not that he cared to change a thing about it. The ball was rolling.

Anna nodded in agreement. "How about this? Talk to me about Sunny Side and I'll stay for a glass of wine."

Was it really as innocent as that? His skeptical side wanted to think that it wasn't, but it'd been a long day. At least he could enjoy a glass of good wine and derive deep satisfaction from admiring his nemesis's little sister. "I'll open it right now."

"So, Sunny Side," Anna said. "They could be an amazing acquisition for LangTel."

Jacob opened the bottle at the wet bar, filled two glasses and brought them to the lacquered cocktail table. He sat near Anna and clinked his glass with hers. "Cheers." Taking a long sip, he studied her lovely face, especially her mouth. He'd only had her lips on his for a few moments, but he knew the spark beneath her composed exterior. She could so easily be his undoing. He hadn't anticipated this beguiling creature resurfacing in his life. Or that she might disrupt the riskiest investment venture of his career.

"Well?" she asked. "Sunny Side?"

"Yes. Sorry. It's been a long day." He shook his head, trying to make sense of the situation. "Is there a point in discussing it? Sunny Side might consider an offer from LangTel, but the problem is Adam. I don't see him wanting to acquire a company I'm so deeply entrenched with and frankly, I'm never getting into bed with him either." Getting into bed with Adam's sister might be another matter. Loyalty was no longer standing in the way.

She nodded, intently focused. "I'll take care of Adam. I just want to know if you can put me in the room with Sunny Side."

"Just so you know, it's about more than money. The founder is very leery of big business. It took months for me to earn his trust."

Her eyes flashed. She was undaunted by obstacles. If anything, it brought out her enthusiasm. "Of course. The technology has limitless applications."

"It will revolutionize the entire cell phone industry." One thing dawned on him—the War Chest's interest in LangTel was with the mind of turning the corporation into a bigger moneymaker once Adam was gone. Sunny Side would be a major player in the industry, so why *not* put the two together? It could have an enormous upside.

"So, can we make this happen?"

Jacob admired her persistence. Among other things. "Only if Adam stays out of it."

"Tech acquisitions is my department. Think of it as doing business with me."

"How long do you think you'll stay in that job?" He'd been surprised she'd taken a job with LangTel at all. She always seemed to hate being in her brother's shadow.

"Not forever, hopefully."

"Setting your sights on bigger and better things?"

She smiled politely. "Yes."

He was relieved that she saw herself eventually leaving LangTel. She'd still make a boatload of money from her personal stock if he was successful with a takeover, and her career wouldn't be derailed. Adam was his target, not Anna. "Okay, well, if we're going to talk about Sunny Side, Adam has to stay out of it. A negotiation requires compromise and he is incapable of that. He hates it when you disagree with him."

"I'm familiar with that aspect of his personality." She ran her finger around the edge of the wine glass, her eyes connecting with his and sending a splendid shock right through him. "I could never get Adam to tell me exactly what happened. Between the two of you."

Although Jacob wasn't certain what made Adam react the way he had, he suspected Roger Langford was at the root of it all. It started when Jacob spotted problems with Adam's central idea for Chatterback, the social media website they were starting. They needed to rethink everything. Adam vehemently disagreed. He brooded, they argued for days on end. Jacob suggested Adam consult with his dad—maybe he could talk some sense into him. The next day, Jacob had been cut out entirely. "I find that surprising. I assumed he bad-mouthed me to anyone who would listen."

"He did some of that, but he mostly just never wanted to talk about it." Anna wound her arms around her waist.

Did he care to venture down this road tonight? Absolutely not. The details were too infuriating—money lost, countless hours, passion and hard work unfairly yanked away. Plus, he couldn't tell Anna that he suspected her father had been the problem. She was likely still grieving him. "I don't want to be accused of trying to taint your opinion of Adam. He is your brother, after all."

"Okay, then at least tell me that you'll put me in the room with Sunny Side."

His mind went to work, calculating. There were myriad ways in which this could all go wrong. Of course, if it went right, that could be a real coup. "I'll make it happen, but this is only because of you. I don't want Adam interfering."

"Believe me, I won't let him get in the middle." Anna took a sip of her wine. When she set down the glass, she laughed quietly and shook her head. "It was bad enough when he was the reason you didn't want me to kiss you."

Two

Adam's fiancée, Melanie, pointed to the dog-eared pages of bridal magazines spread out on the dining table in Adam's penthouse apartment. "Anna? What do you think? Black or eggplant?"

Bridesmaid's dresses. Talking about the dress she'd have to wear for Adam and Melanie's January wedding felt like a speed bump. Anna'd been trying to broach the subject of Jacob and Miami for nearly the entire week, but Adam kept putting her off.

"Do you have a preference?" Melanie asked.

Anna shook her head, setting down her dessert spoon. The chocolate mousse Melanie had served with dinner was delicious, and perfect, just like Adam and Melanie's life—a well-matched couple giddily in love, wedding a few months down the road. "I'm sorry. What were you saying?"

"Classic black A-line or strapless dark purple?"

Anna choked back a sigh. She was happy for Adam and Melanie, really she was, but their wedding had taken over Langford family life. It was the only thing their mother, Evelyn, wanted to talk about. Just to make things especially fun for Anna, her mother usually added a comment about how her first project after the wedding was helping Anna find the right guy. January couldn't come—and go—soon enough.

She loved her brother dearly. Melanie had become a close friend. It was just that it was painful to watch them reach a milestone Anna was skeptical she'd ever reach. At twenty-eight, being hopelessly single in a city full of men who didn't have eyes for women with lofty aspirations, there wasn't much else to think. Most men were intimidated by her family and the job she'd already ascended to at LangTel. It wasn't going to get any less daunting for them if and when she took over as CEO.

"The black, I guess," Anna said. "But you should pick what you want. Don't worry about me. It's your big day, not mine."

"No, I want you to be happy. I think we'll go with the black." Melanie smiled warmly.

Anna really did adore her future sister-in-law. These days, Melanie was the only thing that made being around Adam tolerable, which was so sad. Adam had once been her ally. Now it was as if she had a grizzly bear for a brother and a boss—she never knew what would set him off, and most days, it seemed as if everything did.

She'd assumed she and Adam would lean on each other after their father passed away, but instead, Adam had withdrawn. He'd holed up in Dad's big corner office and become distant. The tougher things got, the more Adam shut her out. She'd been exercising patience. Everyone dealt with death differently. If only he'd trust her with more responsibility, she could lighten his workload and remind him that she was well equipped to take over.

Melanie took Adam's hand across the sleek ebony table, her stunning Harry Winston engagement ring glinting. "I still can't believe we're getting married. I pinch myself every morning."

"Just wait until we have kids," Adam quipped. "Then things will really get surreal."

"You're already talking about children?" Anna tried to squelch the extreme surprise in her voice.

"We are," Melanie answered. "Two of my sisters had trouble getting pregnant. If we're going to have kids, I don't want to risk waiting too long."

Anna nodded. She'd worried about how long she would have to wait. Her friends from college were having kids, some their second or third. On an intellectual level, she knew she had time, but after her dad had died, emotion had taken over reasoning, and she panicked.

Feeling alone while watching Adam move forward with his life, Anna decided she wasn't about to wait for a man to show up in hers. She'd looked into artificial insemination. It was a just-in-case sort of thing—a fact-finding mission. Hopefully, she'd find love and a partner and none of it would be necessary, but at that moment when she'd felt powerless, taking action was the only comfort she could get.

Unfortunately, the visit to the clinic brought a devastating problem to light—a tangle of scar tissue from her appendectomy, literally choking off her chances of conception unless she had surgery. If she didn't fix the problem and she did become pregnant, carrying a baby to term was unlikely. With things crazy at work, Anna hadn't done a thing about it, although she planned to. Some day.

"We aren't going to have to try, Mel." Adam leaned back in his chair, folding his hands behind his head. "If I have my way, you'll be pregnant by the end of the honeymoon."

Melanie laughed quietly. "Did Adam tell you about Fiji?" she asked Anna. "Two weeks in a private villa on the beach with a chef and an on-call masseuse, all while the rest of New York is dealing with gray snow and cold. I can't wait."

Fiji. In January. Anna took a cleansing breath. She hated these feelings of envy. She wanted to squash them like a bug.

"We need to talk about that, because we're going to be away for a full two weeks," Adam said to Anna. "If you think that's too long a stretch for you to be in charge at LangTel, you need to tell me now."

Anna blew out an exasperated breath. "I can't believe you think there's a chance I can't handle it."

Adam fetched a bottle of beer from the fridge and returned to the table. "What about Australia? What if something like that happens when I'm gone? We're still sorting out that mess."

"First off, *we're* not sorting out that mess, I am. And you asked me to make those changes. I was following orders."

"If you're going to be CEO, you have to think for yourself." He took a sip of his beer and pointed at her with the neck of the bottle. "There will be no orders to follow."

How she hated it when he talked down to her like that, as if she didn't know as much about business, when she absolutely did. "And I will do that once you finally hand over the reins." Anna tightened her hands into balls. She was so tired of her dynamic with Adam, constantly at war.

Melanie buried her nose in a bridal magazine. Surely this wasn't a comfortable conversation to sit in on.

"When you're ready and not a day sooner," Adam barked. "You know we're in a delicate position. The company stock is fluctuating like crazy. I keep hearing rumblings about somebody, somewhere, wanting to take over the company."

She'd heard those same rumors, but had ignored them, hoping they were conjecture and nothing more. "Adam, change brings instability. I think you're making excuses, when the truth is that you suddenly have zero confidence in me."

"You don't make it easy when you make mistakes. Half of the board members are old guard. They do not want to see a woman take over the company, no matter what they might say to your face. We have to find the right time."

Anna felt as though she was listening to her

father speak. Was there something about working out of that office that made a person completely unreasonable? "You mean I have to wait until you decide it's the right time."

"You have no idea the amount of pressure I'm under. People expect huge things from me and from LangTel. I can't let what Dad started be anything less than amazing."

Anna kept her thoughts to herself. Adam was struggling with their father's death even more than she was. He might not realize it, but she was sure his iron grip on LangTel had more to do with holding on to the memory of their dad than anything else. Tears stung Anna's eyes just thinking about her father, but she wouldn't cry. Not now.

"I can do this. I thought you believed in me."

"I do, but frankly, you haven't dazzled me like I thought you would."

"Then let me dazzle you. I have an idea for an acquisition after the conference in Miami. That's what I've been trying to talk to you all week about."

"I don't want to spend our entire evening talking shop. Send me the details in an email and we'll talk about it tomorrow."

"No. You keep blowing me off. Plus, I'm starting to think this isn't a discussion for the office."

"Why not?"

You might get mad enough to set off the sprinkler system. "Because it has to do with Jacob Lin. I'm interested in a company called Sunny Side, and he's the majority investor."

Adam's jaw dropped and quickly froze in place. "I don't care if Jacob Lin is selling the Empire State Building for a dollar. We're not doing business with him. End of discussion."

That last bit was so like her dad, and such a guy thing to do, attempting to do away with an uncomfortable subject with male posturing. It insulted every brain cell in her head, which meant it was time to forge ahead. She wasn't about to wait for another time. It might never come. "The company makes micro solar panels for cell phones, phones that will never, ever need an electrical charge."

"Sounds amazing," Melanie chimed in from behind the shield of her magazine.

Adam shook his head, just as stubborn as Anna had imagined he'd be. "No, it doesn't."

"Yes, it does," Anna said. "We're talking about a revolution in our industry. Imagine the possibilities. Every person who ever wandered around an airport looking for an outlet will never see a reason to buy a phone other than ours."

"Think of the safety aspects. Or the possibilities for remote places," Melanie added. "The public relations upside could be huge."

"Not to mention the financial upside," Anna said.

Adam kneaded his forehead. "Are you two in cahoots or something? I don't care if Jacob has invested in a cell phone that will make dinner and do your taxes. He and I tried to work together once and it was impossible. The man doesn't know how to work with other people."

Her conversation with Jacob was fresh in her mind, what he'd said about the end of his friendship with Adam. What if things had been different and they had remained friends? "Funny, but he says the same thing about you."

Adam turned and narrowed his focus, his eyes

launching daggers at Anna. "You spoke to him about this?"

"Actually, I met with him. I told him that Lang-Tel is interested in Sunny Side."

"I can't believe you would do that."

"Come on, Adam." Anna leaned forward, hoping to plead with her eyes. "We would be passing up a huge opportunity. Just take a minute and look past your history with Jacob for the good of LangTel. You'll see that I'm right."

Adam stood up from the table. "I can't listen to this anymore. I'm going to answer emails and take a shower." He leaned down and kissed the top of Melanie's head. "Good night."

"That's it?" Anna asked, bolting out of her seat, her chair scraping loudly on the hardwood floors. "The almighty Adam passes down his decree and I'm supposed to live with it, even when my idea could make billions for the company he won't hand over because he's so concerned with its success?"

"Look, I call the shots. I'm CEO."

Anna felt as if she'd been punched in the stomach. "You've reminded me of that every day since you took over."

"Good. Because I don't want to talk about this ever again. And I don't want you to speak to Jacob Lin ever again, either." He started down the hall, but turned and doubled back, raising a finger in the air as if he'd just had the greatest idea. "In fact, I forbid it."

"Excuse me?" She remained frozen, beyond stunned. "You forbid it?"

"Yes, Anna. I forbid it. You are my employee and I am forbidding you to talk to him. He's dangerous and I don't trust him. At all."

Three

Jacob ended his first conversation with Adam Langford in six years with a growl of disgust, dropping his cell phone onto the weight bench in his home gym. Where exactly did Adam get off calling him? And issuing orders? Stay away from his sister? Keep your little cell phone company to yourself? Jacob had a good mind to get in his car, storm through the lobby of LangTel up to Adam's office and finally have it out, once and for all. Lock the door. Two guys. Fists. Go time.

Jacob leaped up onto the treadmill, upping his pre-set speed of six miles per hour to seven.

Rain streaked the windows. Morning sunlight fought to break through gray September clouds looming over the Manhattan skyline. His long legs carried him across the conveyor belt, his breaths coming quicker, but it wasn't enough. It wasn't hard. It wasn't painful. He upped his speed again. He craved every bit of release he could get—no sex in two months, a powder keg of a job and an infuriating phone conversation with his biggest adversary made him feel as if he might explode.

It was more than what Adam had said, it was the way he'd said it, so smug and assuming. Adam wasn't all-powerful. He never had been, although he loved to act as though he was. Adam did not control him. The suggestion, even the slightest hint that he did, made his blood boil. He'd show Adam. He'd do whatever the hell he wanted. He would get as close to Anna as humanly possible, in any way she wanted to be close to him. If she wanted to do business, they would. If she wanted a replay of that kiss, they'd do that, too.

Jacob quickly finished five miles, every stride

only steeling his conviction that Adam needed to be humbled, big time. He'd felt that way before Anna had come into the picture, and although she had no idea, she'd set off a chain of events that left him fixated on his goal. Adam needed to know what it felt like when someone destroyed everything you'd worked so hard for.

That was merely the business side. There were other unpaid debts. When Adam had betrayed him, he'd thrown away their friendship as if it meant nothing. That left a familiar void—Jacob found himself without a close friend, exactly as he'd lived out much of his childhood and adolescence, shuttled from one private school in Europe to another, never having enough time to fit in.

He'd been a straight-A student, but hardly had to try at all—that annoyed the hell out of the smart kids. He came from unspeakable wealth, but it was new money. He'd had to learn the hard way that there was a difference. He didn't have a notable lineage behind his family name. His father was immensely powerful, but that was in the Asian banking world, not the entrenched circles of old-world high society in England and France. Jacob was left in a no-man's-land, with plenty of money for the highest tuitions, the grades to get into the best schools and nothing to focus on but studies that didn't challenge him in the slightest.

The real shame was that his friendship with Anna became collateral damage when things went south with Adam. Their immediate rapport had shown so much promise. He felt truly at ease with her. He could talk to her about anything, especially his upbringing, something he did not share easily. She always listened. If she hadn't had the same experiences, she still empathized, and she found a bright spot in everything.

The night she'd kissed him, he'd been equal parts shocked and thrilled. He'd been pushing aside thoughts of his lips on hers from the moment he met her. She was off-limits, his friendship with Adam too precious. So he'd had to tell her "no." He'd been sure his bond with Adam would be stronger because of it. But that had been a mistake. Every mistake he'd made because of Adam was an open wound, refusing to heal.

What if he and Anna brought things full circle? For just one night? They could start where they left off with that kiss six years ago, this time without Adam in the way. It would be more than physical gratification. A tryst with Anna would be another instance in which Jacob showed Adam just how little control he had.

Jacob muted the bank of televisions airing global financial news in front of him. He sat back down on the weight bench, picked up his phone and called the founder of Sunny Side. He was open to meeting with Anna, but could they do it upstate? Mark and Jacob had homes thirty minutes from each other. Perfect. Out from under the meddlesome reach of Adam.

He ended the call and scrolled through the contacts until he found Anna. Rational thought and urges warred inside his head. Could he cross that line? He would never hurt her. Business or pleasure—Sunny Side or sex, he'd follow her lead, but they could get nowhere until he set them on the right path.

"Jacob. Hello," she quickly answered, hushing her voice.

Her softly spoken words were much like early-morning pillow talk, bringing a pleasant sensation, a rush of warmth. Perhaps it was the knowledge that his actions would enrage Adam. "Anna. How are you today?"

"Good. You?"

She had to be covering. Adam must've been hard on her when she'd brought up the notion of doing business with Jacob. Too bad for Adam—this call was about Anna and Jacob putting together a deal. No more letting Adam get in the way. "I'm good. I wanted to talk to you about Sunny Side. I spoke to Mark, the founder, and he's amenable to the three of us meeting this weekend."

"Really? That would be fabulous."

Jacob was surprised by Anna's lack of hesitation. She'd spoken to Adam about this—Adam had said as much, and yet she seemed undaunted, unwilling to conform to Adam's wishes. A woman after his own heart. "We'll see how things go. If you two talk and it's not a good match, that's the end of that. But I can't imagine you not hitting it off with Mark. I doubt he'll have a defense for the Anna Langford charm."

That last part was the truth, not necessarily meant as flirtation, although he knew very well it came out that way.

"I could always wave a fat stack of cash in his face," she quipped.

"Coming from you, I'd say that sounds incredibly sexy." Visions of Anna seductively thumbing through a bundle of hundreds materialized. That *would* be sexy. Insanely sexy.

"I'll be sure to run by the bank."

A protracted silence played out over the line. It was partly his fault. He'd really tripped himself up with "sexy." He cleared his throat. "So you're up for the meeting?"

"Absolutely."

How he loved her decisiveness, her fire. It made him want to kick himself for ever saying "no" to her. "We're meeting at my place in Upstate New York if you can make that work. Mark bought a house about a half hour from mine. I don't know about you, but I could really use the getaway."

"Getaway? You and me?"

"Just for a night. It's too far to go for just a few hours. Or at least that's what I say to force myself to take a break from work."

"Oh. I see."

Why was going away with him the one point of hesitation? Was she thinking he was making a pass? He didn't want her to think so. "It'll be like old times. If you're lucky, I might even beat your butt at cards."

"We have to have this meeting and talk hard numbers. That's really important."

He blew out a breath. Maybe it was for the best that she was determined to focus on business. That would make it more difficult for his mind to stray to other thoughts of Anna. It would be trial enough to be alone in the same house. "Of course. Everything you need."

She hummed on the other line, as if mulling over her decision. "Yes. I'll be there. Should I hire a car or is there a flight I can catch?"

"We can ride up together. Text me your address and I'll pick you up early tomorrow morning."

"Oh, okay. Great. Is there anything special I need to bring?"

"Maybe your bikini?" The instant it came out of his mouth, he realized it sounded like a bad pick-up line.

"Not really my go-to for a meeting."

Find a save. Find a save. "And there's nothing like a soak in the hot tub after a tough negotiation."

A getaway. With Jacob. Anna pressed the button to take the elevator down to the lobby of her building. She sucked in a deep breath. Her skin noticeably prickled when she thought about what she was doing and with whom she would be doing it. This was about as wrong as wrong could be—going away to discuss a business venture that was supposed to be a dead issue. Going away with the man her brother despised, the man she'd been warned to stay away from.

But Anna spent every day doing what everyone expected of her and where had that gotten her? Frustrated and running in circles. There was no reward in playing it safe. Of that, she was absolutely sure.

Could she have devised a more tempting plan to make Adam regret ever selling her short? Not likely. So, she'd be spending it in close proximity to the man she had a certifiable weakness for, a man who'd been sure to remind her to pack a bikini. She was strong, or so she hoped.

After she and Jacob had gotten off the phone the day before, the bathing suit talk had sent her rushing to the salon to get everything imaginable waxed as well as getting her nails done. Sure, it was girlish and vain, but if she was going to let Jacob see her climbing into his hot tub, he was at least going to second-guess the wisdom of ever turning her down.

Anna stepped off the elevator. As she made her way to the glass doors, a sleek, black SUV pulled up to the curb. She wasn't sure exactly what make it was, only that several guys eyed it as they walked by, as if it was a supermodel bending over in a short skirt. Jacob rounded the front of the vehicle in a black sweater, jeans and dark sunglasses. Had he managed to get hotter since she'd seen him in Miami? He was as tempting as ever, square-shouldered, as if he was bulletproof. *Damn.*

She ducked into the revolving door with her overnight bag just as Jacob caught sight of her. He came to a halt on the sidewalk, grinning. His magnetism was so effortless. It was in his DNA. He ran his hand through his shiny, black hair and pushed his sunglasses up on his nose. That seemingly harmless sequence of motions left her dizzy. Hopefully she'd get reacclimated to Jacob quickly, desensitized to the ways he could make the most benign action enticing. She had more than a few recollections of staring at his hands while he shuffled playing cards.

"Ready?" His impossibly deep voice stood out amidst the sounds of the city.

"Yes," she answered with a squeak.

He reached for her bag, grasping the handle. Their fingers brushed and her body read it as an invitation, even though her brain insisted it was nothing. Meaningless. Still, if he touched any more of her than that, she was a goner. He opened the passenger door. Something about him standing there, waiting for her to climb in, gave this the distinct feel of a date, even when she was sure it was only because Jacob was a perfect gentleman.

"I'm a little surprised you're driving. I figured you and your driver would pick me up," she said after he'd tossed her bag into the backseat and gotten in on the driver's side.

Jacob shook his head and started the car. The engine roared, quickly calming to a low and even hum. "I figured this made for more quality time to catch up. No prying eyes."

Anna swallowed hard as Jacob expertly zipped into the confusion of cars whizzing by. "Oh. Sure."

"I trust my driver, but he's only been with me a few months and you never know. I've been burned before by people who talk behind my back. This way, it's one less person who knows what we're doing."

She nodded. *What we're doing.* What in the heck were they doing? Tempting fate? Undoubtedly. If Adam found out about this, especially before she had a chance to be out in front of it, he wouldn't merely go ballistic. He would explode into millions of pieces, only after he was certain she and Jacob were in the bull's-eye of the blast zone. "Thank you. I appreciate that."

"Look, the last thing I want is for you to end up in the doghouse with your brother. We have legitimate reasons to explore this business venture, but we need to put some real numbers together before you can entertain it seriously. If this meeting doesn't go well, no harm, no foul. Adam never needs to know it happened."

"Sounds reasonable to me." The covert nature of their trip was appealing for practical reasons, but misbehaving was its own temptation. She was always the good girl, always did what was expected of her. For once she could deviate from plan, even if her confidence about it wavered. She didn't like deceiving anyone, especially not her family.

That didn't change the fact that she had to get Adam's attention and shake him out of the mindset that she wasn't ready to take over as CEO. Jacob had become her very unlikely ticket to doing that. She had to wonder if money was Jacob's only motivation, or if he thought this deal might show Adam that he'd made a mistake by ending their working relationship. He certainly seemed focused on the business aspect. Telling her to bring her bathing suit was probably a slip or Jacob being a good host. It was hard to imagine it was anything else.

There was a big part of her, however, that wished there was something else. She never did well with the idea of possibilities left unexplored. The night she kissed Jacob, she'd already spent many nights imagining what came next, of what it would be like to have his hands all over her, to share the same bed with him. When he'd cut it short, she couldn't help but feel as though she'd been robbed of something. That was difficult to let go.

She glanced over at Jacob as he fiddled with the satellite radio while navigating the snarl of traffic leaving the city. His profile was endlessly enthralling. She could've sat there and studied his strong, dark brows or his uncannily straight nose for hours. That would only lead to the examination of his perfect lips, the way his angular jaw was accentuated by his well-groomed scruff. It would be so nice to trail her finger along the line from his ear to his chin, kiss him again and see if he wanted to explore their unfinished business.

But what if he'd only used Adam as an excuse, a means of covering up the fact that he hadn't wanted to kiss her at all? If she tried anything a second time, he might be honest with her. That would be brutal.

He turned and narrowed his focus on her for an instant, making her heart leap into her throat. "Everything okay?"

She nodded, swallowing back a sigh. "Oh, sure. I was just wondering how long the drive is."

He looked back over his shoulder and sped up, changing lanes like a man who wasn't about to let anyone get in his way. The scent of his cologne wafted to her nose, making her lose her bearings. "Five hours. Four and a half if I can get out of traffic." He reached across and patted her on the leg, the width of his palm and fingers spanning her thigh. "Sit back and enjoy the ride."

She stared down at her lap, the place where he'd left an invisible scorching-hot handprint. Five hours? Alone in a car with Jacob? She'd be on fire by the time they got there.

Four

In the years since he'd graduated from Harvard Business School, the only time Jacob had mixed business and pleasure was right now—taking Anna away for the weekend. Time alone in the car with her had quickly illustrated that being with her made things muddy, messy. Nothing was clear-cut and that made him nervous. Considering the game he was playing with LangTel stock, getting close to Anna was dangerous. It wasn't just playing with fire. It was tantamount to walking a tightrope over an active volcano.

But the fire was so tempting—her sweet smell, the way she pulled out her ponytail and redid it when she was thinking about something. He'd struggled to keep his eyes on the road. The deep blue turtleneck she wore was maddening. His brain wouldn't stop fixating on trying to remember the exact arrangement of freckles on her chest. And then there were the jeans. Sure, he'd held the car door to be a gentleman, but he'd committed every curve to memory, frame by frame, as she'd climbed inside his car.

Finally at their destination, he turned from the main road and stopped between the pair of towering stone pillars flanking the entrance to his estate. Cool autumn air rushed in when he rolled down the window to punch in the security code. Silently, the wrought iron gate rolled aside, granting entry into his retreat, a world that intentionally bore no resemblance to the one they'd left behind in Manhattan. The fall leaves blazed with a riot of brilliant orange and rust and gold. The trees rustled with a stiff breeze, leaves breaking free from their branches, some landing on the hood and windshield, the rest drifting until they came to rest on the white crushed-stone driveway.

The massive house stood sentry at the head of a circular parking area.

"Wow," she muttered, leaning to the side and peering out her window as he parked the car. "It's so gorgeous, Jacob. And huge."

Surely Anna had been to impressive estates, but she seemed quite taken with what he had to offer her for the weekend—pristine grounds, crisp, white clapboards wrapping the spires at each corner of the house, a wide sweep of stone stairs leading to the front door, flanked by hand-leaded windows. His pride swelled. He couldn't help it. He'd impressed her and he was glad that he had.

"The house was built in the twenties. I had it completely remodeled when I bought it three years ago." As much as he loved his job, it was a pressure cooker, and being in Manhattan only exacerbated it. "I figured it was a good invest-ment and I wanted a getaway that would always be here. Something I could depend on. Some-thing comfortable."

Jacob snatched up the keys in his hand and climbed out of the car. He didn't make it around in time to open Anna's door for her, but he was able to grab her overnight bag before she had the chance to do so. He wanted to at least do some things for her. In fact, he'd purposely called the house's caretaker and asked him to give them a wide berth this weekend. There would already be his cook and housekeeper around.

"Seems like a lot of space for one person," Anna said, as they made their way to the front door. "How often do your parents come to visit?"

Family was such an integral part of Anna's life. It was probably impossible for her to fathom an existence that didn't revolve around it. "You'd be surprised." He opened the door and ushered her inside, placing their bags on a bench in the spacious foyer.

"A lot, then?"

He shook his head. "No. Not much at all. Especially not my dad. My mom will come for a weekend once a year, but she's antsy the whole time she's here. I think she probably learned that from my dad." As hard as Jacob liked to work, he had seen his dad take it too far. He made a point of relaxing when he came up here, but that almost exclusively involved getting his hands dirty. Very dirty. He'd have to show Anna his collection after he'd shown her the house.

Anna turned and frowned. "Don't you get lonely up here?"

Jacob was so accustomed to being alone that it didn't faze him at all, but he was smart enough to know that most people didn't live that way. Especially not a Langford. "I won't be lonely this weekend. That's all that matters right now." He chided himself the instant the words were out of his mouth. Why couldn't he answer, "no"? Why was flirtation and leading answers his inclination? He wasn't the guy who had trouble turning off this aspect of his personality. He was usually far more in control.

Anna flushed with the most gorgeous shade of pink. "That's a great way of thinking."

The urge to cup the side of her face and sweep his thumb across the swell of her cheek bubbled up inside him. Stuffing his hands in his pockets was the only way to stop himself. He wasn't about to cross that line. He needed to get a grip and wrap his head around everything he was fighting in his mind. When he'd been irate with Adam, it was easy to imagine getting back at him by seducing his sister. But then he'd picked her up at her apartment and he was quickly reminded of two things—Adam's sister was a woman he cared about, and a path that led to intimacy was not to be taken lightly. A smart man would insist that the risk was not worth the reward, even if the reward did look stunning in her blue sweater.

As in all business, detachment was the most proven tack. For the moment, it meant focusing on his head and ignoring his body. There was a very clear answer to the question of what his body wanted—Anna. He couldn't even fathom what might happen if he made a move. Would she cast away her brown eyes in shyness or would she have the courage to meet his gaze and tell him what she wanted? If he could have anything right then and there, he would've loved to know what she was thinking. Why was she here? What was driving her? Was it really as simple as wanting to broker a big deal? Or was there something else?

He cleared his throat. "Allow me to give you the tour."

Anna nodded and he led the way.

Anna had grown up amidst wealth and splendor, but Jacob's house was truly remarkable—beautifully refinished wood floors, a refined mix of modern furnishings and antiques, every surface impeccable and of the finest quality. Even her mother would've been a bit envious, and Evelyn Langford devoted an awful lot of time and resources to feathering her nest.

They returned to the front door, and Anna assumed they were going to go upstairs to see the bedrooms. Instead, Jacob handed over her coat. "I have something I want to show you in the garage."

The garage? He was aware she knew what a lawn mower looked like, wasn't he? "Okay. Sure."

They walked along a wide flagstone walkway, past the swimming pool and tennis courts. Beyond was an enormous outbuilding. Practically a warehouse, with a keypad entry and a security system Jacob had to disarm once they were inside. He flipped a succession of switches and the lights flickered on, one by one, across the massive room. Anna gasped.

It was an homage to motorized travel—seven or eight very expensive-looking cars, all black, and at least two dozen motorcycles. The entire room was spotless—polished concrete floors, not a speck of dust or dirt anywhere. Chrome gleamed. The aroma of motor oil and tooled leather swirled around her, a smell she'd never anticipated could be so appealing. She'd had men show off collections before—art, autographed baseballs. One guy owned what she'd thought was a dizzying array of antique chess sets. Talk about dizzying—Jacob's display of testosterone-fueled fascination was enough to make her head swim.

"Jacob, wow. I can't even…" Anna paced ahead slowly, Jacob right behind her. She was mesmerized, but afraid to touch the wrong thing. "They're incredible."

They stood before a bike with a worn but polished brown leather seat. "This is my hobby.

Everything is vintage. Nothing built after 1958. Some of them I've bought from other collectors, but quite a few were falling apart when I got them. They were a lot of work, but I love it."

She folded her hands. Jacob loomed behind her, so close. She could feel the measured rhythm of his breaths even when she couldn't see him. "You do the actual repairs?"

"Is that hard to believe?"

She shrugged. "I don't know. I'm just surprised you know how to do it, that's all."

He let out a breathy laugh. "At first, it was the challenge of teaching myself how to do it. I was very motivated to learn. Now it's simply that I don't trust anyone with these. They're prized possessions and that means I keep them all to myself."

"Well, they're just incredible. Truly beautiful. I'm very impressed."

He stepped over to a bike in the center of the front row, swung his long leg over the seat and straddled it. "This one is my favorite. A Vincent Black Shadow. Very collectible." The motorcycle popped back off its kickstand, bounced in place a few times under his weight. His hands—good God, his hands—gripped the handles in a way that said he didn't merely know how to care for the machinery. He knew how to ride.

"Take me out," she blurted.

He smirked, his eyes crinkling at the corner. "It's cold out there. You'll freeze."

"I'll live."

"Have you even been on a motorcycle?" His voice rumbled, low and gravelly.

She had most certainly *not* been on a motorcycle. She'd lived her entire life in Manhattan. Riding on a motorcycle was the sort of thing her parents never, ever would have allowed her to do. As an adult, she'd never had the chance. Nor had she put much thought into how all-out sexy the idea might be until confronted with it.

"No. I haven't. And that's why I want you to take me out." She shook her head slowly, their eyes connecting. His dark stare was like a tractor beam—he could have drawn her across the room with a single thought, not needing to utter a word or even curl a finger. He made her so damn nervous when he looked at her like that, as if he knew how easily he could mold her every vulnerability into something of his own. She didn't have a lot of weaknesses, but there were a few. Did he know that he was one? That look on his face made her think that he did.

"You know what they say about this particular motorcycle?" he asked.

"No clue."

"That if you ride on it fast, for long enough, you're bound to die."

Anna gnawed on her lower lip. What was it about being with Jacob, the man she wasn't supposed to be with, that emboldened her? Because there was no denying that it did. He could've been about to push her over the edge of a cliff and she would've jumped off herself and figured out what to do on the way down. "I'm not scared."

"You realize that if any part of you gets hurt, your brother will have my head."

Anna wasn't much for pain, but she wouldn't mind Jacob wearing her out a little. Or a lot. "So now you're going to use Adam as your excuse?"

He sat back, tall and straight, brushing the side

of the bike's body with his hand. He granted her the smallest fraction of a smile and it made her knees buckle. "When you put it that way, I don't think I have a choice." He pushed the kickstand back into place and climbed off the bike, heading for a tall cabinet in the corner. "Let's find you a helmet and a jacket."

Her mind was at war with itself. *What are you doing? You came up here for a meeting. Shut up shut up shut up. Forget work. Forget the meeting. Who turns down a motorcycle ride with an insanely hot guy?*

"We just need to be back in time for our meeting," she said, as if it would make this sensible if she brought up work.

"That's two hours from now. Plenty of time."

"Okay." Anna trailed over to him, wishing she'd had something smart or sexy or at least sane to say. She felt so overmatched, much as she had when Jacob had come to stay with her family that Christmas. As if he was guiding her, pulling her in, making her his. Except that it had never materialized that time. Was it all in her head? Would it actually happen now? If not, it would be fantastic to know now so she could preserve her dignity by dodging another brush-off.

He turned, holding out a black leather jacket. "Allow me."

She made a one-eighty, her back to him, steeling herself to his touch, sliding her arms into the heavy garment, which weighed down her shoulders.

He patted her back gently. "A little big, but it'll work."

The sleeves were stiff, and she had to work at bending her arms to zip up the jacket. Boxy and clumsy for her frame, it made her feel like a child in a winter coat a size too big. She faced him and her brain sputtered, fixated on the image of him as he put on his own jacket. Dammit. It fit like he'd been born in it, adding a dangerous veneer to his admirable physique. Where did he get that thing? The Absurdly Tall and Broad-Shouldered Men's Warehouse?

He grabbed a shiny silver helmet, but instead of handing it to her, he curled his hand around her head and reached for her ponytail, gently tugging on it as he pulled out the hair tie. She was so shocked, it was as if he'd pulled her breath out of her lungs at the same time. Her tresses collapsed around her shoulders. He was close enough to kiss. His mouth was right there—lips as tempting as could be, the moment resembling the one that preceded her ill-fated attempt at seduction. They'd been standing in nearly the same posture and stance. Why couldn't he have taken her hair in his hands that night? Why couldn't he have decided that she was more important than Adam?

"One of my old girlfriends always complained that it hurt to wear a ponytail that high with a helmet."

Talk about ruining the moment. He *would* have to bring up other women, wouldn't he? Of course he'd gone on with his life, including his romantic one, after they parted ways years ago. He was smart. He hadn't wasted untold amounts of time wishing for someone he couldn't have.

She nodded. "I never would've thought to take down my hair."

He zipped up his motorcycle jacket, which was the sexiest meeting of metal teeth in the history of apparel fasteners. "If you want to know the truth, it's just that I find that moment when a woman shakes out her hair after riding on the back of my bike particularly sexy."

Was that his way of throwing down the gauntlet? Issuing a dare? Because she sure as heck could whip around her hair. She might not be the purely confident seductress, but that much she could handle. The raw anticipation of the ride ahead returned to her veins, pumping blood from head to toe.

"Ready?" he asked, climbing onto the Black Shadow.

He pressed a button on a key fob and one of the wide garage bay doors began to open. The crisp air rolled inside, but she appreciated the cooling effect on her ragged nerves. Jacob put on his helmet, then his sunglasses. Lastly, he pulled on a pair of black leather gloves.

"Yep," she answered, sidling up to the bike. She realized then that it wasn't the idea of the ride making her nervous. It was the idea of touching him. Then again, this gave her the perfect excuse, and if this was as close as they got all weekend, she'd find a way to live with it and later weave it into a super hot fantasy. She pulled on her helmet, adjusted the chin strap, and grasped his shoulders as she straddled the bike behind him.

He started the engine. The bike rumbled beneath them. "Hold on tight," he yelled back to her.

She wrapped her hands around his waist tentatively. She didn't want to be so hopelessly obvious. Better to wait until their speed warranted a stronger grip. The next thing she knew, they were moving, albeit slowly, as he turned to close the garage door. Then he sped up, rounding the outbuildings, chugging down the gravel driveway to the road, opening the gate ahead of them with another click of the fob.

He came to a dead stop at the road, balancing them with his foot on the blacktop as the gate closed behind them.

"You can go a little faster, you know," she yelled.

"That was gravel," he called back. "You want fast?"

Anna gulped. "Yes."

"I'll show you fast."

He revved the gas, still keeping them in place. The power of the engine had her body trembling. The bike lurched and they hurtled ahead like a rocket. They flew down the narrow state road, picking up speed, much faster than they'd gone in his car. Maybe it only seemed that way because she no longer had the protection of a steel cage around her. The momentum of the bike pulled her away from him, and she tightened her grip around his waist, clamped her thighs to his hips. Her shoulders tensed, but at the same time, she felt freed. It was the oddest sensation. Laughter and elation bubbled out of her. The wind whipped at her jeans, but the jacket kept her warm. As did Jacob. Very warm.

The engine popped and roared whenever he changed gears. Masterfully, he handled the bike, leading them through a curve. She grabbed him even tighter as he leaned them into the turn, defying the laws of gravity. The way his shoulders shifted, maneuvering the bike through the treacherous bend, was unspeakably hot. She loved seeing him so in control. One wrong move and they'd both be gone. In that moment, she couldn't imagine wrong. He was infallible. Invincible.

They continued for miles, on narrow, serpentine roads. He took her through a small town with a roundabout, the changing leaves fluttering around them, people milling about from a coffee shop to a farmer's market, bundled up in hats and scarves. She felt as cozy as could be, as if she was curled up in front of the fire. The fire of Jacob. Once they got back to the open stretches of rural road, he took off like a bat out of hell again. He got cocky on a long straightaway, weaving back and forth. If only he could have seen the mile-wide smile on her face. He'd earned his macho moment. And good for him for claiming it.

Much too soon, the road returned to where they'd started, only this time, from the opposite direction. He took the gravel drive leading to his house slowly again, expertly guiding them into the safety of the garage.

Anna was catching her breath, adrenaline coursing through her. She unclasped her hands from Jacob's waist, but her arms were heavy under the weight of the jacket and they dropped. Dead center. Between his legs. She yanked back her hands as if she'd touched a hot stove. In some ways, that was exactly what she'd done. She gripped his shoulders to climb off the motorcycle. Embarrassment flooded her. She could only imagine what he must be thinking. Was he wondering if that was her awkward attempt at a pass? Because she was wondering the same thing.

Five

Composure was no longer possible. Jacob gripped the motorcycle handlebars, but only to steady himself. Anna and her slender, feminine hands had just stirred primal urges from the depths of his gut. It had been building in the car. The motorcycle ride brought it closer to the boil—her arms coiled around him, her clasped hands pressing into his stomach when he went faster, her thighs pressing into his hips, squeezing him when he took the turns. And then there had been the noises she made—muffled shrieks and cries of excitement. How was a man supposed to live through that without his body responding?

And then she'd touched him there.

He closed his eyes to take the edge off, but the reality was that he wanted her, and he was fairly certain that she wanted him. Was that brush across his crotch her way of sending a message? It didn't seem at all like Anna's style— she was subtle and demure, rarely so bold, but she'd been testing limits of late, with her brother and her career. Was she testing Jacob? He had to find out. Every drop of blood circling below his waist was making it impossible to let the question go unanswered.

He dared to open his eyes. She'd removed her helmet. He'd missed the moment when she took it off, but the result was worth it. Her hair was mussed—tousled, nearly disheveled, not at all its usual glossy neatness. He liked it. He liked it a lot. He could picture the rich, dark color against the white sheets of his bed. Her cheeks were flushed and rosy; he hoped not from the brisk autumn air, but from the thrill of the ride, the rush of being close to each other.

He cleared his throat as he climbed off the motorcycle. Now to figure out a way to get the ten or so paces to the gear cabinet where she was standing—his jeans were too snug to make walking a casual affair. He used his helmet to shield himself.

"That was so much fun. Thank you," Anna said, breaking the silence.

He wasn't in the mood for skirting things anymore. No purely polite response to her gratitude would come from him. "Isn't that what a guy does?" He eased out of his jacket and hung it up in the cabinet.

"Does what?" Anna furrowed her brow, climbing out from under the pounds of leather she was wearing.

"Try to impress a woman by showing off." He placed his helmet on the shelf, then turned to face her square-on. It took considerable effort to obscure his edginess. His attraction to her hadn't manifested itself this strongly before. His mind was racing to keep up.

She cocked an eyebrow. Her warm brown eyes flashed. "Is that what that was?" Her lips remained parted after the question, the flirtation only provocation to the devil on his shoulder.

"Yes." He scanned her face, waiting for one more sign—something that said it was a good idea to do what he wanted to do.

A warmth washed across her face. "If that's you showing off, you can do that all you want."

And there it was. He sucked in a deep breath of resolve and erased the gap between them. He clasped both hands around her neck, pushing his fingers into the silky hair at her nape and lifting her mouth to his, collecting what he wanted with a tender, but insistent kiss. Her lips were even sweeter than he remembered, the kind of dessert that makes you lick the spoon over and over again, craving one more taste.

"Tell me to stop," he said, not relinquishing the grip he had on the back of her neck. His thumb caressed the smooth skin below her ear.

"What?" Her eyes were half open, breaths heavy enough to hear.

"Tell me you want me to stop." His heart raced, part of him begging her to say that she wanted him, part of him knowing that it would be easier on them both if she stopped this right now. Being with Anna, as badly as he wanted her, would be pouring fuel on the flame that had dogged him for too long. "Tell me that you don't want me to kiss you."

Her mouth went slack, eyes wide as the day was long. "I can't," she muttered.

His heart was fighting to pound its way out of his chest. Whatever it was that she couldn't do, he wasn't sure he wanted to know what it was. "You can't what?"

"I can't tell you to stop because I don't want you to."

A wave of relief crashed over him. One hand went to her elbow, his fingers tracing the underside of her arm until he reached her palm. "Good. Because I don't think there's any way I can."

He snaked his hands around her waist and she popped up on to tiptoes, planting her arms on his shoulders. He didn't even have to kiss her—she was all over him. As if he'd told her she'd earn a million dollars for every second they didn't come up for air. Their tongues wound together in an endless circle. Their noses bumped as she tilted her head and came in for a different approach. She flattened her stomach against him, and he responded by lowering a hand to her bottom and tugging her hips closer to his.

The metal door of the cabinet clanged against the frame when she pushed him into it. He was still trying to keep up with what was happening, trying like hell not to fixate on where it was going. Would their first time be in the garage? That could be insanely hot. But where? Concrete floor? Tool bench? He tensed for a second. He wanted it to be better than that. If they were only going to have one night, one weekend, he wanted them both to remember it. He quieted his mind. This was not the time for overthinking. His body relaxed. That only made him more susceptible to Anna's fire.

She hitched her leg over his hip as if she knew exactly what she was doing. Either she had far more experience than he'd ever bargained on, or she was going on pure enthusiasm. He hoped for the second, that this was her response to him, not just another time with another man.

"Do you have any idea how long I've dreamed

about this happening?" Anna asked. Her voice was all sweet desperation.

His body came to a complete halt. *Dreamed?* Did this mean more to her than he'd banked on? If they were going to have their fling, they couldn't make love in a car or on a tool bench. He needed to make this right, not merely salacious and reckless.

"Believe me, I thought about our kiss a few times over the years."

"Just a few?" she asked, seeking eye contact. Her eyes were clear and intent, searching his face.

He couldn't tell her it had been more than that. It would only make things more complicated. There were enough dangerous feelings between himself and one Langford. "Let's not talk about the past anymore. I'm tired of it."

"I don't want to talk anyway."

Jacob caught sight of the clock on the wall. *Oh, no.* "Anna. Our meeting is in ten minutes."

She blew out a deep breath. "It is?" She lowered her head and shook it. An adorable groan leaked from her mouth. "Okay. I guess it's time to get to work."

* * *

So much for Anna's resolve that this trip was going to be about business and absolutely nothing else. She'd had about as much self-restraint as a toddler in a toy store the minute Jacob kissed her. She still couldn't believe she'd pushed him up against the cabinet door. Then again, she'd waited a long time for Jacob.

But there was work to be done. She sat and smiled politely as Jacob and Mark got situated in the living room at Jacob's. A fire crackled in the fireplace, the late afternoon sun cast a warm golden glow through the windows. Jacob had his arm spread out along the back of the chocolate brown leather sofa, his leg crossed, his other hand playing with the stitching at the end of the sofa arm. He laughed quietly at something Mark said, and glanced over at Anna with a look that made any sound in the room turn to a low hum. It was a look born of recognition. He wanted her and he sure as hell knew that she wanted him. There were no more questions of that basic intent. The real question was who would be the first to break down. Was she sitting inside the fireplace? It sure felt that way.

Her entire body warmed, in exactly the way a fire builds—a spark, dead center in her chest, became dancing licks of flame in her shoulders and belly, and the heat rolled right through her, making her face hot and her toes just as naturally off temperature. That kiss—that single, brain-chemistry-altering kiss, was more gratifying than any physical encounter she'd had with a man in years. What if more happened? What if clothes started to come off? Would she pass out? She might.

"So, Mark," Jacob started, again sliding a shy smile to Anna. "I'd love it if you could give Anna an overview of what you envision for the future of Sunny Side. I think that'll be a good start and then we can see if partnering with a corporation like LangTel could be a good option."

Mark shifted in his seat, stroking his hipster beard, not looking entirely sold on the premise of corporate anything. He struck her as a man who'd be a stickler on the finer points of an arrangement between the two companies. This deal, if it happened, would require more than the right amount of money. A day ago, Mark's reticence would have unhinged Anna to no end. Today, it was more of an annoyance. If he didn't want to be here, why didn't he just say so? Then she and Jacob could get back to business of an entirely different nature.

Mark nodded and started on his song and dance about Sunny Side. Anna listened, taking notes on projections and plans for future products, ideas he had for the launch of the technology, product integrations and applications. Adam was a damn fool for letting his rift with Jacob stand in the way of this deal. Of course, the fact that he'd ignored the financial upside was testament to how much he hated the man she'd just kissed with reckless abandon in the garage.

"Anna? Do you have any questions for Mark?"

She was on deck. It was time to make her case. Jacob might be distracting the hell out of her, but she needed to focus. "I don't. I've had a chance to look over these numbers and if your projections hold true, I'd say that Sunny Side can pretty much write their own ticket. So the real question is, how do we make that work within the structure of LangTel?"

Mark leaned forward and set his elbows on his knees. "Look, Ms. Langford..."

"Please. Call me Anna."

"Anna. You have to understand that I run a company of two dozen employees. Our product has come to fruition so seamlessly because we're a tight-knit group. Our company culture is immensely important. My worry is that a giant like LangTel will swallow us whole or dismantle us until there's nothing left."

"Let me assure you. We have no interest in dismantling your company. The dynamic of your team is crucial to your success. We will absolutely keep it intact."

"How can you make promises like that? Isn't your brother CEO? I've heard he can be ruthless."

Jacob shot her a sideways glance, as if to remind her that Adam's reputation was of his own making, not Jacob's, and he wasn't wrong. Adam liked knowing that some people feared him.

"Actually, Adam's business thinking is very much in-line with yours. He's started two immensely successful and innovative companies from the ground up..." She stopped herself. One of those two ventures was the one Jacob and Adam had started together, the very source of the rift that made everything such a mess. Her stomach sank. What must Jacob think of what she'd just said? That she was hopelessly callous? She had to recover from her gaffe. "At the end of the day, whether your company is big or small, everyone wants to retain the dynamic that brought you success. Nobody wants to see someone else come in and dismantle what you've worked so hard for."

Jacob cleared his throat and Anna felt horrible. Bringing up his history with Adam had been a mistake. He'd said it himself in the garage. The last thing he wanted to talk about was the past.

Six

Jacob and Anna bid their goodbyes to Mark as he walked out to his car. The brisk night air filtered into the foyer. With a quiet click, Jacob closed the door. They were alone.

"Well? What did you think of Mark?" he asked, bending over to pick up a stray leaf that had been tracked into the house.

Anna stifled a sigh of appreciation for his backside. The man knew how to work a pair of jeans. "I like him a lot. He seemed open to some of the things I suggested, so that's good." Considering where Anna's mind had been that whole time, it was a wonder she'd been able to glean that much from the meeting.

"Good. Definitely good." He nodded, holding the orange leaf by the stem as if he didn't know what to do with it.

"Yep." The air was charged with anticipation. They both knew where this was going. But no one was doing anything about it. Should she throw herself at him? That was as close to formulating a plan as she could come. "Pretty color." She pointed to the foliar evidence of the fall weather, resorting to painful small talk.

Jacob opened the door again and tossed the leaf outside. A new rush of cool air caused her to shudder. Perhaps it was nature's way of punctuating the fact that this time, he didn't merely close the door. He locked the deadbolt.

"Are you cold?" He dropped his chin, stepping closer, working his way into her psyche with an intense flash of his eyes. His hand gripped her elbow. Energy zipped along her spine.

Finally—touching. Nothing skin-to-skin yet, but at least someone had given in. Anna was hyperaware of her breaths, her galloping heartbeat, the rotating sway of her body in his presence. This wasn't that different from the moment after the motorcycle ride, except then, they'd had to break the ice. She was glad to be done with breaking. Now on to melting. "I caught a chill. I'm okay."

He smiled. "You're so cute when you're deflecting."

"What do you mean?" Even perplexed, her heart flitted at the mention of cute.

"You'll do anything you can to take any and all focus off of you."

She twisted her lips, trying not to fixate on his—the swell, the color, the memory of the way it felt when they were on hers. Why wasn't he kissing her again? Was he going to wait until she started things? "If I do, I never noticed it. It must just be my personality." She wished she could've come up with a sexy answer to the question, but there were too many urges to manage, like the one that told her she'd be a lot happier if he wasn't wearing that sweater. Or those jeans.

"I just find it interesting. Your brother is the complete opposite."

If Anna knew anything, it was this—if he didn't kiss her in the next two seconds, she would go off like a grenade with the pin pulled. "Let's leave Adam out of this. In fact, let's pretend he doesn't even exist."

"Are you flirting with me by describing my Utopia?" His eyes toyed with her. He was reveling in every second of their game.

Her mouth went dry. That kiss in the garage hadn't quenched a six-year-old thirst. It left her wanting more. "And what if I am?" She popped up on to her toes, gripping his shoulders to steady herself. "What if I did this?"

She closed her eyes and went for it—her lips met his, in a kiss that made it feel as if she was no longer standing. There was a millisecond of hesitation from him before his tongue sought hers. Every atom of her body celebrated in a chorus of delight and relief. She shifted her forearms up on to his shoulders, dug her fingers into the back of his thick hair. His lips—soft and warm and wet, became more eager, seeking her jaw and neck. His arms wound tightly around her, pulling her against him, nearly lifting her off her toes.

His hand snaked under the back of her sweater,

conveying what she'd been so eager to know—he wanted clothes to come off as badly as she did. His fingers fumbled with the bra clasp, which was so adorable. He was so smooth. It was nice to know he couldn't make the entire universe conform to his will.

"Here. Let me," she muttered. Now flat-footed, she lifted her sweater over her head then clutched it to her chest. "Everybody's gone for the day, right?" It would be so like her to undress while the gardener was watching.

He laughed, a flicker of appreciation crossing his face as he plucked the sweater from her hands and tossed it onto the foyer bench. "Yes." Leaning closer, he poked his finger under one of her black satin bra straps, popping it off her shoulder. "It's just you and me and this big house."

His words didn't merely prompt a rapid wave of goose bumps—they were about to become a permanent feature of her complexion. She bit down on her lip. If this was going to happen, it would be good. She reached behind and unhooked her bra, but left it for him to take off. "Tell me you want me to stop."

"Tell me you want *me* to stop." He kissed the curve of her neck—the most sensitive spot, the one that made her want to squeal with delight.

"No stopping. Please, no stopping."

He didn't tear his gaze from her as he slid the other strap from her shoulder. He dragged the garment down her arms slowly. His vision sank lower. "You are too beautiful to have anything less than exactly what you want. Tell me what you want." Gripping her rib cage with both hands, his thumbs caressed the tender underside of her breasts, as he lowered his head and gave one nipple a gentle lick.

The gasp that rose from the depths of her throat sounded like a lifetime of frustration being cut loose. She dropped her chin to her chest when he did it again. She loved watching him admire her this way, knowing that she turned him on. "I want you. Right now."

"Upstairs," he muttered.

Before she knew what he was doing, she was off her feet and in his arms, feeling tiny, like she weighed nothing at all. He marched up the stairs and she clung to his neck, desperate to kiss him again.

The hall to his bedroom seemed to stretch for miles. Neither of them said a thing. Their heavy breaths carried the conversation instead. They reached their destination, a grand room with vaulted ceilings and windows overlooking the grounds. He set her down gently on the enormous four-poster bed, smiling.

He lifted his sweater over his head. The soft, evening light showed off the incredible contours and definition of his chest and abs—perfectly smooth, no hair except for a narrow trail below his belly button. His shoulders were far better than any item of clothing had ever suggested. Not even the motorcycle jacket did them justice—square and broad, begging for her touch.

She sat up and flattened her hands against his firm chest, his skin warming her palms. With her arms raised, he cupped her breasts with his hands. She would've dropped her head back in pure ecstasy if she wasn't so anxious to have his mouth on hers again. As if she'd spoken her wish, he bestowed a long, reckless kiss…hot and wet and magnificent.

She was dying of curiosity to know what the rest of him looked like. She unzipped his pants and pushed them to the floor. She dipped her fingers beneath the waistband of his gray boxer briefs, shimmying them down his trim hips. He kissed her again, and she wrapped her hand around his length, relishing the forceful groan that he made into her mouth.

He urged her to lie back, kissing her bare stomach. She watched as he unbuttoned her jeans and wiggled them south. His eyes were on her body as if he were entranced. Everything between her legs was eager for attention. Her entire body tensed with anticipation. "Touch me, Jacob. Please." The words had wandered out of her mouth, the thoughts in her head trickling out.

He tugged her panties down, casting his dark eyes up toward hers as his fingers met her apex. She couldn't let go of her grip on his head as he rocked his hand back and forth. It felt impossibly good to be at his mercy—wanted, desired. The pain of the past washed away like the tide erases writing in the sand. Their gazes locked, and it was as if she could see more of him, parts that he obscured, the vulnerable things he had hidden from her.

The pressure was building, the peak within her grasp too soon. "Make love to me," she said. How many times had she imagined this? Hundreds, and it hadn't come close to matching the real thing.

He dotted her stomach with soft, open-mouth kisses, firmly gripping her waist. When he rose to his feet, he opened the top drawer of a tall, dark-wood bureau. He ripped open the foil packet and handed her the condom. She wasn't about to ruin the moment with mention of the reasons they might not need one. Plus, she liked the idea of focusing on him, just as he had on her.

He stretched out next to her, the most magnificent creature she'd ever seen—strong and muscled, but graceful and lean. He dropped his head back when she wrapped her fingers around him and rolled on the condom. When he returned his sights to her, he looked as if he wanted to consume her, heart and soul.

She arched her back, welcoming him as he sank into her, slowly, carefully, with a reverence she'd never expected or experienced. Her mind was a swirling vortex of thoughts and sensations, the most powerful of which was that she'd suspected he would feel wonderful, but not like this. She couldn't have prepared herself for it feeling this good.

He rolled his hips when his body met hers. It built the pressure in her belly quickly, her breaths coming faster now. Her hands roved over the muscled contours of his back, trailing down to his glorious backside. His kisses were deep and long, matching the steady and satisfying rock of their bodies. She wrapped her ankles around his waist, wanting him closer. Deeper.

She placed her hands on the side of his face, keeping his lips to hers. She wanted to be connected with him like this when she unraveled. Her mind shuffled images—the motorcycle ride, the first real kiss, the moment when he looked at her in the front hall and she knew, with complete certainty, that he wanted her. Everything inside her began to uncoil. She was ready to let go of it all, even the past, and succumb to the bliss she'd waited so long for.

Anna was so close. Jacob could feel it, sense it in every fitful movement of her body. He was fighting to stem the tide, but it wasn't easy. Concentrating on her face was the only way to do it, a beautiful distraction from the energy doubling in his belly.

Her breaths came in frantic bursts. Every sound she made was sweet and sexy, but she nearly blew his mind when she called his name, clutching his back and digging her fingers into his skin. She tensed around him, her body grabbing on to his as if she might never let go.

Deliberate thought was gone. Tension clenched his legs and stomach, pure instinct took over. A blissful smile spread across her face. Breaths shallow, strokes longer and harder. Now faster. The pressure threatened to burst. Anna bucked against him. She fought for it just as eagerly, until finally his body gave in to the pleasure. It barreled through him like a freight train.

"Oh, no," he blurted, stilling himself on top of Anna as the swells ebbed in his body. He'd never had this happen before, but it wasn't hard to guess what it was. He'd felt it. "The condom broke. Don't move."

Anna wrapped her legs around him even tighter. "No. Keep moving. You feel so good." Her voice was catlike, a purr, a fitting match for her reaction. She didn't seem the slightest bit concerned about what he was now panicked about.

"Anna. The condom. It broke. And I just came. Did you not notice?" He pressed one hand into the mattress and slowly began to lift his hips away from hers. What now?

"Oh." She shook her head as he got up from the bed. "I guess I didn't notice."

"Yeah, this is a problem." He rushed off to the bathroom to clean up. "This is a huge problem," he muttered to himself, discarding it and washing his hands. It was one thing to exact revenge on Adam by taking his sister to bed. It was quite another to go and get her pregnant. Plus, a baby? No way. He was the last guy on the planet who had any business becoming a dad.

He stepped into his boxers and rushed back to the bedroom. He could make out Anna's gorgeous curves even in the dark. She'd climbed under the covers, partially covered, lying on her stomach and patting the spot on the bed next to her.

"I missed you," she murmured.

He blinked several times in complete confusion. "I was gone for two minutes. And aren't you worried? There's a very good chance you and I just made a baby."

She shook her head as he eased back into bed next to her. "I'm almost entirely certain that we did not make a baby. Don't worry about it."

Even with the way things had just gone wrong, being that close to her completely naked form had everything in his body stirring again. "Care to fill me in? Maybe I missed that day in health class."

"Can't you just take my word for it?"

"What? You're on the pill? Then why did you let me use a condom?"

She took a breath and buried her face in the pillow.

He rolled to his side, placed his hand in the center of her back. Why did she not understand what a big deal this was? "Anna. What is going on? Will you talk to me, please?"

She finally turned to look at him. "I can't get pregnant."

"What?"

"Or at least not until I get some of my plumbing fixed."

"I'm sorry. You've lost me."

She rolled over, pulled the sheet up over her chest and sat up in bed. He hated the fact that something he'd said made her want to cover up, but he did need to know what in the world she was talking about.

"A fertility doctor told me I can't conceive. I'd gone to talk to him about artificial insemination."

"You're twenty-eight years old. Why would you think about doing something like that?"

He watched a wave of embarrassment cross her face. It nearly took his breath away. He eased closer to her, craving her touch, her smell.

"Losing my dad really made me think about having a baby. About how much I want that in my life at some point."

"Oh." It was hard to imagine ever feeling that way, but lots of people did. Most people, in fact. Or so it seemed.

"All I could think was what if I never find the right guy? Being a female executive is tough. Most men let their ego get in the way."

He had to wonder what sorts of men she'd dated, but he wasn't about to ask. There was no point worrying about that particular obstacle. He'd never get past the barrier of Adam. "I hadn't considered that."

"I've never been serious enough about anyone to want to have a child. And losing my dad underscored how important my family is to me. My whole life revolves around them. Adam and Melanie are building a future together and…" Her voice wavered and she looked up at the ceiling. "This is the world's worst pillow talk. I'm sorry."

He hated seeing her upset. He tried to imagine a scenario in which he could share something like this, something so deeply personal, the sort of thing that left a human hopelessly vulnerable. He gave her a lot of credit for having the courage to be so open. "It's okay. You should tell me about it, if you want to."

"Really? Why?"

He took her hand in his. It wasn't meant as romance, but his inclination to comfort her was strong. "Because I care."

Anna explained everything her doctor had told her about scar tissue and surgery and how that affected her ability to get pregnant. He listened intently, saddened that she'd had to go through that. She clearly cared a lot about having a child. Why else would she have gone to a specialist about it?

"What did your mom say?" he asked.

"I never told her. I never told anyone." The wobble in her voice was back, the one he hated hearing.

If she'd never told anyone, that meant he was the first. The weight of that wasn't easy to bear. Here she was, in his bed, after giving him the most precious thing she could give to him, and now she was baring her soul. He never harbored guilt over a business decision, but his secret weighed on him. He was trying to engineer the takeover of her family's corporation, and she had no idea. What if that came to light? She would never, ever forgive him. And why should she? "Why didn't you tell anyone about what the doctor had said?"

"I wasn't sure I could talk about it without crying."

He was glad she'd been able to hold back tears. He didn't do well when a woman cried. He never knew what to do or say other than give a hug, which he knew didn't fix a damn thing. "But the doctor said it could be fixed, right? With surgery?"

"Yes, but the point was that I just wanted something to be right, to be easy. Everything over the last year has been a nightmare. This was supposed to be my way of looking to the future. I guess I felt a little defeated."

"So we didn't just make a baby."

"We didn't just make a baby."

Relief washed over him again. No baby. Good. Things were tangled enough. Now he just had to deal with his own internal conflict over the LangTel takeover plan, and that might require action on his part. He was excellent at keeping the business and personal separate, and in this case, he'd clearly allowed the two to commingle far too much.

"Are you feeling better now?" she asked. "You were pretty panicked there for a minute."

He laughed quietly. He had indeed let it get the better of him. "I'm fine. Although I wish you would've told me about this earlier. We could've skipped the condom all together. I'm clean. I get tested every year for my physical. Plus, I've never not used one, so it would be virtually impossible."

"You've never felt what it's like without one?"

He shook his head. "Never worked out that way. It can't really be that different, can it?"

A mischievous smile crossed Anna's face. It was so sexy. She scooted closer, until their thighs were touching. She kissed him, sending vibrations through this entire body, especially the parts they'd just been discussing. She took his hand, twined her fingers with his. "I've heard that it's very different."

"Very?" he asked between kisses. His body was ready to discern this for himself.

She climbed on top of him, straddling his hips. "Why don't we test the theory?"

Seven

Jacob finished off his third cup of coffee. Two was his limit, but he hadn't slept at all. It was difficult with a woman in his bed. It was partly sexual distraction, but there was another side to it. Something wouldn't allow him to relax enough to give in to real sleep.

He placed his mug in the sink and strode down the hall to the foyer, where Anna was waiting. "I'll be ready to go in a minute. I need to take care of something in the garage."

"Okay." Anna nodded, smiling thinly. Things were definitely awkward between them now that it was the morning after. How could they not be strained? They'd crossed a line that might've been better left uncrossed, however much they'd both wanted to do it.

He hurried out the door and around back to the garage. He'd deliberated about waiting and making his phone call after they returned to Manhattan, but he had to do it now. He couldn't sit in the car with her for five hours feeling even worse about his secret. He needed absolute privacy, and he wasn't about to kick Anna out of the house. That meant the garage.

He had to take steps to clear his conscience. Could he go through with a LangTel takeover at this point? Even if he and Anna never ended up taking this any further? The answer was a surprising, but decided "no." The guy with the killer instinct for business rarely changed his mind and he never undid his own work, but he was sure. He couldn't hurt Anna. Not after what they'd shared. Even if this weekend had to be the logical end, it wouldn't erase their most intimate moments, and he didn't want to forget them anyway. He wanted to keep them in his head for as long as possible.

He entered the garage and closed the door behind him. He wasted no time pulling out his cell to call Andre, his closest ally in the War Chest. He had to end the campaign against LangTel, even if it might be a tall order. His fellow investors were astute, shrewd, and skeptical to a fault. They would want to know why he was backing off, and he couldn't tell them the real reason. He couldn't tell them that he'd seduced a woman who'd gone and seduced him right back.

"Jacob. What's up?" Andre answered. "Not like you to call me on a Sunday."

"I know. I wanted to talk to you about the LangTel deal. I'm out." He held his breath, not offering any reasons. With his investment record, he could sometimes get away with only a mention that he was making a move and others would follow suit. The why wasn't always necessary.

"You're what? Are you insane? Why would you do that?"

Crap. So he would have to offer an explanation. The cult of personality would only get him so far today. "I don't think the upside is there like we thought it was. And it's such a huge undertaking. We could be knee-deep in this for a year. Or longer. Do we really want that? Do you want that much money tied up like that?"

"With that kind of payday? Yes. Don't forget, you aren't the only person Adam Langford has pissed off over the years. A few guys are eager to knock him down a peg or two."

Everything that had seemed so perfect a few months ago was now quite the opposite. "Isn't the notion of revenge a little outdated? Don't you have better things to do?"

"You seemed pretty damn motivated by revenge that night in Madrid when we first talked about this."

Jacob was skating very thin ice right now. Andre was absolutely right. Jacob had pushed them all. Hell, he'd not only rallied the troops, he'd riled them up. "I can't spend my life worrying about Langford. I'd rather wash my hands of it. And him." That much was the absolute truth, however much he was unsure of his feelings for Anna.

"I don't know what to tell you," Andre said.

"You want out. I'm still in. I can't imagine the other members bailing."

Jacob pursed his lips. How could he have thought for even a second that he might get out of this easily? He'd put a nearly flawless master plan in place. All he could do now was control his own holdings, make a few more phone calls and try to convince some others. Otherwise, what could he do? This train he'd put on the tracks had momentum of its own. "Well, obviously I can't tell you guys what to do. All I can do is tell you that I'm out. I'm moving on to greener pastures. Greener pastures with less of a headache."

"Suit yourself, Lin. I don't see any way any of these guys are going to back down any time soon. Plus, there's talk of a new investor in the mix. A big hitter with very deep pockets."

His mind raced. This was news to him. "A new member? Nobody spoke to me about this. I have say over who joins the group."

"This guy apparently has no interest in joining the group. But he already has extensive holdings in the company and is keenly interested in a takeover. Probably just one more person who hates Adam Langford."

Jacob threaded his hand through his hair, the most colossal headache he'd ever had making his eyes burn. "And no idea who this guy is?"

"None. Right now, it's just talk. I have to ask why you would even care? Even if you pull your money out of the deal, you'll still get the fun of seeing LangTel and Adam Langford taken down. That's gotta be worth something."

Funny how the appeal of seeing Adam destroyed had taken on a pall, all because he'd given in to his desire for Anna. How could he even think about moving forward with Anna when this was all going on? He couldn't. It would be reckless and stupid and worst of all, unconscionable. Forget that her brother despised him—he couldn't begin things with an enormous secret hanging over his head. It would never work. That left him only one option. He had to back off with her. If she wanted to pursue things, she'd have to let him know, and then he'd make a decision. For now, he'd have to play it cool.

"Okay. Thanks. We'll talk soon." Jacob hung up and shoved his phone back into his pocket. So much for being a financial wizard. That wasn't going to keep him warm at night.

Anna couldn't sit in the house anymore. She needed fresh air, so she made her way outside to the driveway and set her overnight bag next to Jacob's car.

The notion of the end of their getaway was all too depressing. Last night had shattered her expectations. Just thinking about the things they had done together, his touch against her skin, every white-hot kiss, made her tingle. They'd flipped on a switch and completed a circuit, but that could be turned off just as easily, couldn't it?

She felt as if he'd answered the question mere moments ago, when he went out to the garage to spend some time with his beloved motorcycles. He'd patted her back on his way out the door, like a pal—as a buddy would do. He'd been distant all morning. It was hard not to take the hint. Last night was in the past. Today, he was moving forward.

She kicked a pebble into a puddle. It had rained at some point in the middle of the night, which left behind a grayish-blue sky with only the wispiest of white clouds. They would have a gloomy ride back to Manhattan, a fitting precursor to what was waiting for her when they got there—family, responsibilities that were more important than a fling. She didn't want to think about it too hard. She wanted to be back in Jacob's bed, curled up in the sheets, pillows cast aside, the rest of the world an afterthought.

So if this was a one-time occurrence, could she be content with that? She caught a glimpse of Jacob as he came out of the garage. The answer was clear as she watched the way he moved. One night would not be enough. In jeans and a gray sweater, clothes that were nothing special on any other man, he was stunning. He lowered his sunglasses, which had been nestled in his thick head of hair. Not being able to see more of him, in every sense of the word, would be such a disappointment. But was that realistic? Considering the circumstances, she feared it was not.

"I need to grab one more thing inside," he

called to her from the flagstone walkway in front of the house.

"No problem. Take your time," she answered.

A muffled version of her cell phone ringtone sounded. *Who's calling me on a Sunday morning?* She fished it from the bottom of her bag, her stomach flip-flopping when she saw the name on the caller ID. Talk about an abrupt jerk back to reality. Adam. She walked away from the car with a finger jammed in her ear. "Adam. Hi. Everything okay?"

"Hey there, Anna Banana. How are you?"

Anna was about to ask if he was feeling well. He hadn't called her by that nickname in years. "I'm good. What's up?" Paranoid thoughts whirred through her brain. Did he have some way of knowing where she was? Of what she was up to? Every bold feeling she'd had yesterday about throwing caution to the wind was now haunting her; it enveloped her with a crushing sense of guilt. She wasn't the girl to sneak around, to hide things from her brother.

"I feel badly about our talk the other night. I was going to call you yesterday, but Mel and I were doing all sorts of wedding stuff. I'm really sorry about the way I spoke to you."

"That's nice, Adam, but you seemed pretty certain about what you were saying at the time."

"I know, but I was caught up in the heat of the moment. I don't want you to think that I don't want you in place as CEO. I do. I definitely do. And I believe in you. It's just…it's been hard. I think you know that."

Had he called to apologize or was he searching for validation? "I do know that. This has been hard for me, too."

He blew out a deep breath. "Look, Mel and I had a long talk last night. I swear, she's so good at figuring out what's going on with me. It's uncanny. I realize now that losing Dad has been much more difficult than I imagined. I knew it would be tough, but not this bad. And the pressure at work. Well, I think I just haven't been myself."

She hadn't quite expected he would come to this realization, ever. Adam had a real affinity for being detached when needed. The pain of losing her dad sat squarely in her chest. It was somehow more pronounced now, realizing that it weighed on Adam just as much. "I know it's been hard. I should've been more patient with you. I know you're doing your best."

"And I realized just how hard I'm being on you, which is so stupid on my part. You're my biggest ally. You're the one person I know I can trust with anything and I'm shutting you out. It's not only stupid, it's not fair to you."

The one person I can trust. The words echoed in her head. And here she was, hours away, with the man her brother had told her to stay away from. "Thank you for saying that."

"So, starting tomorrow morning, you and I need to get together our plan for moving you in as CEO."

It felt as if her heart had just stopped. Was he really saying that? Was he really willing to finally move forward? "We do?"

"Yes. You know, the board of directors is never going to be happy. If I sit around waiting for them to fall in line, you'll never get to take the job you want and I'll never get to return to what I want to do."

Jacob emerged from the house. The smile on his face was everything she wanted to see, while everything she wanted to hear was coming at her over the phone from her brother. She should've been happy, but she knew full well that these two things did not peacefully coexist in the real world. There was no having both.

"Does this mean you've changed your mind about Sunny Side?"

He groaned, making Anna regret even bringing it up. "I don't want to dismiss your idea again. Let's keep an eye on it. Maybe Jacob will take himself out of the mix. I refuse to touch it before then."

"Ready?" Jacob asked, walking around to her side of the car and opening her door.

"Did you say something?" Adam asked.

Inside, she was begging Jacob to please not say another word. Her heart pounded in her chest. This was far too messy. She had to get off the phone right away. "I have to go, but thanks for calling. I really appreciate it. A lot."

"I have confidence in you, kiddo. I really do. I

just had to pull my head out of my rear end for a few minutes."

She sighed. How she'd longed for this moment—to hear Adam say that she was right about something, about anything, that he had confidence in her. "Thank you. That means a lot."

"See you at work tomorrow."

"Yep. See you then."

Anna put her phone back in her purse. Was she the worst human being on the planet? It felt that way. At best, she was a rotten sister for taking up with Jacob and pursuing Sunny Side behind Adam's back.

"Everything okay?" Jacob asked.

"Yes. Just fine." She nodded and climbed into the car, her conversation with Adam replaying in her head. *You're the one person I can trust.* Was it time to climb out of her dream? To keep Jacob where he was—a fun, amazing fling that had come to an end? The answer seemed clear. She'd scratched the itch and now she had to remain loyal to her brother and her own dream job. She'd worked so hard, and it was presuming a lot to even wonder if Jacob was interested in more. He'd been withdrawn all morning.

He started the car and turned on a news talk station. "I want to get caught up on the financial news. Back to work tomorrow morning, you know."

Anna leaned her head against the car window. *Back to work.* "Yes. I know."

Five hours later, they were pulling up in front of her building. "Let me get your door," he said, reaching for the handle on his own.

"No. Hold on." She grabbed his forearm. "I feel like we should talk." She probably should've brought this up during the ride, but she'd chickened out every time. Maybe this was better. At least she had an escape.

Jacob shut off the radio and turned to her. "Yes. Of course."

"I had a really wonderful weekend," she started, already feeling remorseful about what she was about to say. It was the smart thing to do, the right thing to do. It was also the last thing she wanted to do.

"Good. I'm glad. I did, too."

"It's just that..." she sighed deeply. "I like you a lot, but we need to be honest with ourselves. It probably wasn't the smartest thing in the world, considering that we have my family to contend with. I don't see Adam changing his mind any time soon, possibly ever, and my family is really important to me. I just think it will cause a rift that won't be good for me. Or you, for that matter."

"I see." He took his sunglasses out of the cup holder and put them on. "Whatever you want, Anna. You won't get an argument from me."

Was he hurt? Disappointed? His voice was so cold, his tone so aloof, it was impossible to know, but she had a pretty good guess. The night before, everything she'd dreamed of all those years ago, had been nothing but a one-night stand to him. "Okay. Great. I guess I'll talk to you at some point? About Sunny Side?"

He nodded, looking straight ahead through the windshield. "I'll call you if I have any information to share."

"Perfect." She climbed out of the car, closed the door and didn't look back.

This was for the best, but it felt absolutely wretched.

Eight

Telling Jacob "thanks, but no thanks" was the hardest thing Anna had done in a very long time. Four days later and it felt downright stupid.

"Still nothing from, you know, him?" Holly asked, setting a salad down on Anna's desk. They'd taken to eating lunches together in Anna's office since the executive dining room was no fun. Rumors of a LangTel takeover were rampant, but if it was happening, the perpetrator hadn't come to light.

"Shhh," Anna admonished, leaping out of her seat and making sure her door was firmly closed.

"It's not like I said his name." Holly dug into her own salad as if they were discussing the five-day forecast.

"Sorry," Anna whispered, heading back to her desk. "It's just, you know. If Adam found out, he would not be happy. You're literally the only person on the planet who knows about it."

"I feel so privileged to have this information that could get me fired."

"I'm sorry. I hope this isn't bothering you to know. I just had to tell somebody or I was going to go insane. And like it or not, you're my best friend."

"Don't worry. I'm very good at keeping my mouth shut."

Anna sighed. "To answer your question, no, I haven't heard from him, and it's been four days. I don't know why, but I can't stop thinking about him." Of course she couldn't stop thinking about him. It'd been an aeon since she'd felt so alive. But she'd made the sensible decision, choosing to put her career and family at center stage. Those were things she could rely on. Those were things that couldn't be yanked out from under her. After the last year, she needed to know that she was standing on solid ground, even if this particular patch of land still left her wanting more of Jacob.

"Sex will do that to a person, you know," Holly quipped. "Especially if you've gone long enough without it."

It was more than sex, though. She couldn't bring herself to utter those words, especially not to Holly, the woman of zero filter, but it was the truth. Anna hadn't had that kind of connection with a man, well, ever. Perhaps it was the shared history between herself and Jacob, everything she'd spent years anticipating and thinking she'd never have, but it felt even more elemental than that. They fit together—shared dreams, similar mind-sets and aspirations. The physical fit was certainly impossible to ignore. In bed, the fit was mind-blowing. "I guess. Not much I can do about it, though. The drama of my family is too much, and he seemed all too ready to agree."

"Men and their axes to grind. Two women would never allow it to get this bad. They'd smile to each other's faces and do that phony nice speak, then bad-mouth them the minute the other person turned their back. It's much more civilized if you think about it."

Talk about uncivilized—one of Anna's co-workers had uttered Jacob's name in a meeting the day before, and Adam literally kicked the guy out of the meeting. No explanation, just an invitation to get the hell out. He'd softened his approach with her, but he was still being extraordinarily hard on everyone else.

Anna was picking through her salad when her cell phone lit up. Jacob's name popped up on the screen. She dropped her fork into the bowl.

"Who is it?" Holly asked. "You look like you just saw a ghost."

"It's Jacob."

"What are you waiting for?" Her voice was at a near-panic. "Answer it."

Anna wiped her mouth with a napkin and picked up the phone. What in the world could he be calling about? Nothing about their circumstances had changed. She stifled the hope that rose in her chest, that he was calling because he had to see her.

"Jacob, hi." She brandished her hand at Holly to shoo her out of her office, but Holly just sat back in her chair. Anna bugged her eyes. "Please go," she mouthed.

"Fine." Holly feigned sadness by jutting out her lower lip and begrudgingly got up from the chair.

"Is this a good time?" Jacob asked. Even when he was being entirely too businesslike, his voice was so sexy that it shook her to her core.

"Yes. Of course."

"I didn't want to assume, since you're at work, but it's important and I didn't want you to hear this from anyone else but me."

Her heart began to beat furiously in her chest. "Hear what?"

"Sunny Side is going to have to go on hold. The patent has been delayed and there's a design flaw they have to work through. It's pretty routine with a technology like this, but it could be another few months until a sale is in the mix. They want to put their best foot forward with whomever they partner with, and I've advised them that that's a sound strategy."

Anna took in a deep breath through her nose. She fought her disappointment that he hadn't called about something personal. At least he had what might end up being good news—a delay could be fantastic for her. By the time Sunny Side was ready to sell, she might be in place as CEO and she could make the call. "I see. Well, I appreciate you keeping me up to speed on things."

"I hope you don't feel like our weekend was a waste of time because of this."

A waste of time? Does he feel that way? "Of course I don't. It was an amazing trip." There were hundreds more things she wanted to say to him, but could she make that leap? Could she even hint just how badly she wished they could do it all over again? And should she even cross that line again? "It was great. Both personally and professionally."

"Good. I'm glad to hear that you still feel like that."

Her mind was whirring like a broken blender. Why did it feel as if he was calling about more? And if he was, why wasn't he just getting to it?

It wasn't like him to tiptoe about things. "You didn't really think that I only cared about Sunny Side, did you?"

"No, I didn't. I just wanted to be sure." He cleared his throat. "Anna, I have to tell you something else. I'm actually glad that the delay with Sunny Side happened because it gave me an excuse to call you."

"You don't need an excuse. We're friends, aren't we?"

"Friends with a very complicated set of circumstances."

That much was indeed true. It didn't change the fact that she was hopelessly drawn to him. "So just call me whenever. You don't need an excuse." A long silence played out on the other end of the line. Had she nudged things too far? Was he now trying to find a way out of this phone call?

"Okay, good. Because I'm calling you right now to tell you that I can't stop thinking about you."

She smiled so wide that she witnessed the rise of her own cheeks. Her heart had apparently gotten the memo—it sprang into action by thumping her pulse in her ears. "Really?" Anna dug the heel of her pump into the office carpet, wagging herself back and forth in her chair, ultimately propelling herself into a lazy spin.

"It's especially bothersome when I'm trying to go to sleep."

She dropped her foot, stopping the chair. "Oh. I see."

"I just keep thinking about what it was like to be with you. I keep thinking about touching you, kissing you. I want to be able to do that again."

"You do?" Her mind went there—a gloriously wild confusion of every sexy moment they shared together…the way his butt looked when he walked away from her, the way his mouth went slack when she did something that pleased him. And then there was the dark, intense stare he gave her when he had her pinned beneath his bodyweight, taking his time, making sure she relished every subtle move he made.

"Yes, I do. I also would appreciate it if you would stop asking questions and give me some indication as to how you feel about this. Right now I feel like I'm having one-sided phone sex."

If she blurted out everything going through her head right now, he wouldn't get a word in edgewise for a week. "I can't stop thinking about you, either." Something about making the admission was so freeing, however vulnerable it made her.

"Go on." His voice rumbled over the line.

"And I'm having the same problem. I can't sleep. I just lie there in the dark and replay everything that happened last weekend."

"Good." His declaration had a confounding finality to it.

Anna furrowed her brow. "Good?"

"No more questions. I'm sending a car to pick you up at five."

"I have a meeting at four-thirty."

"Is it important?"

What was it about the velvety quality of his voice that made her want to not merely throw caution to the wind, but send it through a paper shredder? Taking directives from a man was not on the list of things she enjoyed doing. In fact, she usually went out of her way to avoid it, but this was different. She not only knew what he was implying, but precisely what he was capable of. "I'll reschedule."

"That's my girl."

My girl. The words sent electricity zinging through her body. "Where are we going?"

"We aren't going anywhere. You're coming here."

Oh crap. I'm going to have to run home and change.

"And, Anna. Bring a toothbrush."

Nine

Jacob had never done anything quite so weak, but all bets were apparently off when it came to Anna. He'd managed four whole days without calling her. Why give in now? He knew from experience that the first forty-eight hours were the worst, when you know it's in your own best interest to stay away from someone.

In the case of Anna, it had only gotten harder after those first two days. It was like he was being starved for air, which was disconcerting. He couldn't focus on his work. He needed more of her and he needed her now. Damn the consequences, however complicated. Damn the fallout, too. He needed her insistent hands grabbing his body, her strong and graceful legs wrapped around him. He needed to smell her and kiss her, hear her laugh. He needed his fix.

He had to temper the romance. This was a rabbit hole for him emotionally. He didn't let many people into his life and when he did, he didn't want them to waltz right out. That wasn't the point of trust. If you believed in someone, if you wanted them in your life, they would stay. There was no telling how long Anna would be able to stay, or even if she would want to.

Tempering romance aside, he knew he couldn't start an ongoing no-strings-attached thing with Anna. Even when strings meant the Langfords on some level. This left him with a very narrow tightrope on which to balance, at least for the foreseeable future. The War Chest had closed ranks, forging ahead with the scheme he'd planted in their heads. He refused to regret doing it, but he sure as hell wished he could turn it around. If he could just find someone willing to back down, the rest of them might follow, and that would mean one less thing hanging over his head.

He glanced at his watch. Anna would be here any minute and that made his nerve endings stand up straight and tall, pinging electricity throughout his body. The anticipation brewed an unholy cocktail of adrenaline and testosterone in him. He could only imagine what it would be like when he finally saw her. When he could finally kiss her again, feel her come alive beneath his touch. That was the response he cherished—when she allowed herself to be vulnerable, when she surrendered to him and he could feel and see the tangible results—quivers, shakes and trembles.

He walked out into his kitchen and removed a bottle of champagne from the fridge. Cliché? Maybe. But Anna did deserve at least one or two trappings of romance. He wasn't about to let that go completely unaddressed.

The knock at his door sent his pulse embarking on a similar staccato rhythm. He retained his composure, fairly certain that it was the smooth, in-control Jacob that she lusted after. The one she wanted to take to bed.

He opened the door and had to fight the impulses of his jaw. This was not the time to do nothing more than stand there, mouth agape, like an idiot.

"Hi." Her grin was equal parts flirtatious and shy. Her cheeks flushed with that gorgeous pink, a slightly paler shade than her lips, all of it hopelessly inviting.

"Hello yourself." He ushered her in, shutting the door.

He followed her into the living room just off the foyer and helped her with her coat. His eyes zeroed in on the view—her black, sleeveless dress was tailored within a whisper of her figure, hugging every gorgeous inch. Good God. Was he still standing? The thing he admired most about her in that dress was that a woman like Anna could get away with wearing something like that to a meeting. Granted, a meeting where every guy in the room might have an impossible time focusing. Her toned legs looked even more tempting in black sky-high heels. Note to self:

bring Anna to an important meeting someday. She'll make the deal.

"You look absolutely gorgeous," he said, craving her touch. He tossed her coat over the back of a chair and gripped her elbow. The electricity between them was obscene, like an out-of-control Tesla experiment. He was surprised he couldn't see the sizzling current arcing between them.

"Thank you." Her head dropped to the side, only a fraction of an inch, but he loved to see her soften to him like that, to give him a subtle indication that he was on the right track. "You don't look half-bad yourself." She stepped closer, still needing to look up at him in killer heels. He might have to beg her to keep them on the whole night.

Her hand pressed against his chest, smoothing the fabric of his suit jacket. He watched her, smiling, their eyes connecting. It looked as if there was a fire blazing behind hers—hot and intense. Which one of them would give in first? He had no idea, only that for once in his life he knew that he'd still be the winner if he was the first to show his hand.

"I missed you, Anna. I know we said that this wasn't a good idea, but I missed you. It's as simple as that. I missed standing close to you and looking at you and thinking about all of the things I want to do with you. The things I want to do to you."

Her lips parted ever so slightly and a gentle rush of air passed them. It was the sound of pressure being released. "I couldn't stop thinking about you, either. Every time I thought of the reasons we should stay away from each other, I just kept coming back to that original thought…"

He was reasonably sure of what she might say next, but he wanted to hear her say it. "Thought of what?"

"Of you and everything I was missing by staying away."

Perfect. "So now what?"

Her hand hadn't left his chest. She bowed into him, placing her other hand opposite it. Her fingers played with the knot of his tie. "We have the whole night ahead of us. Maybe we just need to see what happens."

He smiled again, this time much wider. It was hard not to be incurably happy around her. "Like what happens when I do this?" He snaked his hand around her waist and settled it in the curve of her lower back.

"Mmm." Her lips traveled closer to his. "I think the next thing that happens is this." She tugged his tie loose, watching his reaction. She flicked open the top button of his shirt, taking liberties again. "Oops. I took two turns in a row."

"Taking advantage, I see," he murmured. This game of undressing, however compelling and sexy, would need to be seen to a quick conclusion. He wanted her naked. Now. He reached up for the zipper, pulling it down the center of her back as she made quick work of his shirt buttons. He longed to see that stretch of her skin, the one he'd kissed a week ago. He turned her around, admiring her porcelain beauty as it contrasted with a black bra and as he lowered the zipper further, lacy panties. He eased the dress

from her shoulders, savoring every sensory pleasure—her smell, the heat that radiated from her,
her smooth skin as he dragged the back of his
hand along the channel of her spine. Her presence didn't merely have him primed, he was already teetering on the brink.

The garment slumped to the floor and she cast
a sexy look back at him, her eyes deep, warm,
and craving. "You made a big jump ahead there."

Hell yes, he had. And he'd do it again in a
heartbeat. He grasped her shoulders and pinned
her back to his chest, wrapping his arms around
her waist. She craned her neck and he kissed her,
hard. He cupped one of her breasts, the silky
fabric of her bra teasing his palm as she tightened beneath his touch, her nipple hard. Their
tongues tangled and Anna righted herself, turning in his arms. He took off his jacket and tie as
she unhooked his belt and unzipped his pants in
a flurry. He wrangled himself out of the rest of
his clothes with one hand while keeping her as
close as possible with the other. He wouldn't let
go of the kiss either—she'd cast aside sweet for
an edge that he couldn't ignore.

With a pop, he unhooked her bra, and didn't bother with the seduction of teasing it from her body. He cupped her breasts, molding them in his hands, his mouth seeking one of her deep pink, firm nipples. The gasp that came from her when he flicked his tongue against her tight skin was music to his ears.

She kicked off one of her shoes and then the other and stepped out of her panties.

Her beautiful bare curves heightened his awareness of how badly his body was driven to claim hers. There was no way he'd make it to the bedroom. He sat on the couch next to them, half reclining, and reached out his hand. "Come here. I need you."

She smiled and cocked an eyebrow, taking his hand. "Are you that impatient?"

"Yes. And we have all night." The breath caught in his chest as he watched her carefully set her knee next to his hip and straddle him. The sky outside was quickly falling into darkness, but the light was just bright enough to show off the dips and hollows of her delicate collarbone. He traced his finger along the contours.

"Calling you this morning was the best thing I've done in a long time."

"I couldn't agree more." She smiled, dropping her head to kiss him. Her silky hair brushed the sides of his face. He was almost sorry he didn't have the visual of the moment she took him in her hand, guided him inside, and began to sink down around him. A deep groan escaped his throat as her body molded around him, warm and inviting. He wanted to be nowhere else.

She settled her weight on his and they moved together in a dance he never wanted to end. It buoyed his senses, made him appreciate her beauty and essential nature even more than before. She rocked her hips into his, over and over again, as they kissed and his hands grasped the velvety skin of her perfect bottom. Her breaths quickened and before he knew what was happening, she was gathering around him in steady pulses. She sat back, their eyes connecting for an instant before she gave in to the sensation, closing her eyes and knocking her head back. He closed his own eyes and the relief shuddered out of him, each passing wave invisibly bringing them closer.

* * *

Anna collapsed back on the bed, her chest heaving with fast and heavy breaths. Jacob clutched her hand, struggling just as much for air. She glanced over at the clock. It was after midnight. They hadn't stopped for much more than a snack and a glass of champagne since she'd arrived a little after five. How much stamina could one man have? Was he trying to prove a point? Because he had. And then some.

She was spent. Wonderfully, gloriously spent. It struck her as a summertime kind of exhaustion, the kind she'd experienced as a kid, up at the Langford family beach house. After swimming all day, sun-soaked, stomach sore from laughing too hard, you were absolutely starving. You would take your first bite of food at dinner and be sure that nothing had ever tasted so good.

That was Jacob. Nothing had felt so good before him.

"Can I just take the chance now to apologize for what happened that first time we kissed?" he asked. "It's pretty clear that was the wrong decision."

She rolled to her side, smiling, despite the unpleasant nature of the topic he'd just chosen to introduce. "You don't have to pretend that you wished things had ended differently. It's okay. I'm a big girl. Plus, you made up for it tonight."

"Don't you think I regret it? What exactly did I turn you down for? A friendship that would ultimately turn into the worst thing in my entire life."

Had she gone through years of pain over the wrong decision? She didn't want to believe that. It would be more comforting to go with the theory that everything happens for a reason. "As much as it hurt to have you say no, I have to admire the reason you did it, even if it didn't turn out the way you would've liked."

He stared up at the ceiling, seeming immersed in thought. Was his rift with Adam something deeper than warring over a business decision? She'd always assumed that Jacob's side of things was about the embarrassment of being publicly shut out of his first major business deal, about losing his cut of a big payday. Was there something else?

"I'm a loyal person, Anna. You have to understand that. If I let someone into my life, they're there for a reason. I don't do it lightly."

And there was her answer. "So it's not just about business. It's about losing the friendship, too."

He was quiet again, but she didn't want to interrupt whatever was running through his head. The intensity of his reservation was one of the things that had first drawn her to him. She bristled with curiosity, wondering what exactly his brilliant mind was choosing to ruminate over. She placed her hand on his stomach—he tensed at first touch, but just as quickly she felt his muscles give in to her. He grasped her hand and raised it to his mouth, kissing her fingers tenderly.

Anna felt equal parts exposed and protected. Did he feel the same? Was it the power of the afterglow, or was there more? Even when her brother had insisted that she couldn't trust Jacob, Anna couldn't buy into it. Her gut told her that she could. Plus, she didn't want to believe that the man who'd once turned down sex out of respect for a friendship would do anything less than the right thing. She might be inching closer to the edge of a treacherous place, but she wanted to believe that Jacob would tug her back if she put herself in the path of true danger. He had to. She didn't want to think anything less of him.

"I don't want to burden you with the minutiae of what happened between Adam and me," he said, breaking the silence between them. "We're having such an amazing night. I don't dare mess with that."

She propped herself up on her elbow and gazed down into his face. He was so gorgeous that it boggled the mind sometimes, even more so at this moment, when he'd given her a glimpse of how deep the waters running through him really were. Would she ever fully know those depths? If she were to live in this instant for all eternity, she wanted nothing more than to drown in them, sink to the bottom and never come up for air. There was so much to learn—she hungered for it.

But was it the right thing to do? To dive in, knowing the repercussions? Was it her weakness for him that was making her so eager to do the foolhardy thing? Maybe. Probably. Did she care? Not really. There were no guarantees, regardless of the situation two people found themselves in. It was up to them to find a way. No one could do it for them.

He rolled toward her and placed the softest, sexiest, most intimate kiss on her lips, plunging her into the sea she longed to get lost in. His hand wound to the small of her back, fingers drawing delicate circles against her skin. She could do nothing more than press against him— the inches between them felt so absurd. Pointless. Of course they should be together. Even if it might bring everything crashing down.

Ten

Life quickly became a beautiful blur, weeks of weekend trysts and countless late-night rendezvous. Sneaking around wasn't Anna's preference, but she couldn't deny herself the glory of time with Jacob, so as difficult as it was, they took great care to keep things a secret.

It was working for the most part, although there were times when it was touch and go. One day in the office, Adam had asked why she was so tired. Was she coming down with something? She couldn't tell him the truth, that she and Jacob had been up until all hours making love, intermixed with eating ice cream in bed and watching bad reality television. So she'd said that she simply wasn't sleeping well. It wasn't a *real* lie, or at least not a big one, but the tiny untruths were beginning to hang over her like a dark cloud.

"What do you want to do tonight? What if we went out for a change?" Jacob asked over the phone as Anna sat at her desk.

"You know we can't do that. What if someone sees us together?" It was the awful truth, but tonight it was more of a convenient excuse. She glanced at the clock on her laptop and began packing up her things. If she was going to beat Jacob back to his apartment, she needed to leave now. She'd scrambled to put together a small birthday surprise—nothing too elaborate, but she hoped he would enjoy it.

"Anna. We can't do this forever. We need to get out of the house now and then. Not that I don't want to leave you tied to my bed. I do."

She smiled. It was hard not to—he was so good at working in the comments that reminded her how much he wanted her. Her most girlish tendencies lived for those moments. "You're right. We'll talk about it tonight. Your place?" He *was* right. They couldn't do this forever. Something would have to give, and that something bore a remarkable resemblance to her brother.

"Yes," he answered, seeming a bit exasperated. "I'll be home by seven. You have your key?"

"I do." He'd given it to her a few days ago, as a "just in case." She wasn't entirely sure of what that meant, but it made a surprise dinner possible.

"Anna?" he asked, with a sexy, leading tone.

"Yes?" she replied, knowing full well what he was about to say.

"I miss you."

She smiled, absentmindedly trailing her fingers along her collarbone. *I miss you*—three silly words they'd been saying to each other for a few weeks. It was one of their many secrets, the things they hid from the rest of the world. Were they a placeholder for "I love you"? Those particular three words hadn't come yet, however much she hoped that they would. They'd sat on her lips several times, but would he return them? Just like the ill-fated kiss years ago, the thought of that kind of rejection was too much. Wait, she'd told herself. It would happen. They would find a way. She had to believe.

"Miss you, too. I'll see you tonight."

She told her assistant she had some errands to run and tried to ignore the guilty feelings that came along with ducking out of work early. After retrieving a carrot cake from the bakery around the corner from Jacob's building, she let herself into his apartment.

It was certainly strange to be in his place on her own. What would it feel like to come home here? Even with the spaciousness of her own apartment, it didn't have the sprawling splendor of Jacob's penthouse, nor did it have the magnificent Central Park view. She could be more than comfortable here. She could be happy. That would be a wonderful life, if she could ever get to that point. She sensed Jacob was proceeding with caution and how could he not be? Her brother hated him. That would scare even the most formidable man away.

A half hour later, she was making good progress with dinner. She wasn't the world's greatest cook, but she could hold her own with pasta and a salad, and it wouldn't be the same if she'd ordered takeout. Luckily, Jacob was easily pleased. A big guy who worked out five days a week, he'd eat virtually anything you put in front of him, especially if accompanied by a glass of good wine.

Even though the dining room table could easily accommodate ten, she set it for two, placing them side-by-side at one end. She found some candles in the buffet, dimmed the lights. Then she returned to the kitchen to finish the preparations. He was only a few minutes late when he strolled into the kitchen.

"What's all this?" He smiled, seeming genuinely perplexed.

Anna rushed over to kiss him—a surreal moment, for sure. Was that what it would feel like to be husband and wife? She might not have much time to get dinner on the table if and when she became CEO, but she enjoyed this glimpse of domesticity. It felt especially comfortable with Jacob. "It's a surprise. For your birthday."

His brow furrowed. He now seemed even

more confused. "How did you know it was my birthday?"

"You had your passport out on the dresser the other day and I wanted to sneak a peek at the picture."

"So you were snooping." He smirked, suggesting he wasn't entirely disappointed in her.

"A little. But that's beside the point. I wanted to do something nice for you. Honestly, I'm a little surprised you never told me about it in the first place."

"I don't really celebrate my birthday." He loosened his tie. "I never have."

"Really? Why?"

"I spent a lot of time away from my parents as a kid. They were always doing their own thing, I was away at boarding school. It just doesn't mean much when you get money wired into your bank account and a phone call."

It was about the saddest thing she'd heard in a long time, but she didn't want to dwell on the negative. She took his hand and led him into the dining room, where she sat him down and poured him a glass of red. She held out her glass to clink with his. "Happy birthday." Something about the sentiment fell short, like she was supposed to add something about their future or that she loved him.

As to what tomorrow held, or even a month from then, she didn't know. As to the question of love, she knew in her heart that she did. He understood her in ways that no one else seemed to—he appreciated her aspirations, he encouraged her, he commiserated when she'd had a difficult day at work. He was always so focused on her, everything she wanted and needed. No one had ever done that, and he made it seem so effortless. Even better, he accepted her affection unconditionally. He never had an agenda outside of being with her.

It was perfect. *He* was perfect, or at least he was perfect for her. But that made their situation all the more frustrating, stuck as she was between him and her family.

She served their salads and took the seat next to him. How could he have gone his whole life not celebrating his birthday? Her heart felt unusually heavy—birthdays had always been a big event in the Langford household. Always. She wanted him to have that, to have everything she'd had.

"Maybe today can be the start of a new birthday tradition."

He offered her the faintest of smiles. "That's a nice idea."

The start of a new tradition. Did Anna really mean that? Did she see a future for them? Because as incredible as it was to be with her, it felt as if the universe was conspiring against them. It was only a matter of time before the War Chest takeover surfaced.

He ate his salad, listening to Anna talk about her day, feeling more guilty with every bite. Hours before, the War Chest had staged their coup against him—ousting him from the group for daring to push them so hard, vowing to continue with their hostile takeover of LangTel. They'd done to him what he'd once hoped they could do to Adam. Being on the receiving end of vengeance wasn't fun. These people were dangerous, all deep pockets and determination. Experience told him that it didn't take much else to be successful. Not even luck.

Anna served the pasta, which might've been one of the most delicious things he'd ever tasted—ziti with Italian sausage, white wine, saffron and arugula. She'd found the recipe online after having taken note of how much he loved those particular ingredients—so thoughtful of her, and yet he couldn't truly enjoy a single bite. Watching her, the sweet smile on her face, thinking about the effort she'd gone to. She'd planned this incredible evening for him, and he'd planned to destroy the company her father had built. What kind of a monster was he? Had getting back at Adam really been that damn important? Had his father messed him up so badly that his so-called business brilliance was capable of ruining lives?

He had to find a way to stop it—sell every asset he had, pull together a new group of investors to help him. Something. There had to be a way. Because the truth was that he was absolutely falling in love with Anna. He'd known it for weeks now. Hell, he was fairly sure he'd fallen for her during the motorcycle ride. But he couldn't confess his true feelings for her until the takeover was squashed. That was no way to start a life together, with a secret of epic proportions lurking in the shadows, about to reveal itself at any time.

After they finished Anna's meal, she brought in a cake and serenaded him with "Happy Birthday" in her slightly off-tune voice. It was corny and adorable and not at all the sort of attention he'd ever had before he'd met Anna—sweet, genuine and thoughtful. Then she gave him his gift—a gorgeous pair of perfect-fitting black leather gloves.

"They're handmade," she said, watching with excitement as he tried them on. "I called a motorcycle shop out in Queens and talked to the owner, so I knew what kind to get."

"Thank you. Thank you so much." His heart ached, so overwhelmed with this show of generosity from Anna.

"You forgot the card." She flipped over the gift box and removed a small envelope taped to the lid.

His eyes couldn't be torn from her as he opened it. Where had she come from? Was this all a dream?

For Jacob,
There's no one I'd rather be on a motorcycle
with. I'll be the one holding on tight.
Love, Anna

He nodded, struggling to manage the emotions welling inside him. *Love, Anna.* He loved her. She was so warm and giving, so beautiful, inside and out. He wasn't even sure he deserved to be in the same room with her, let alone ever have a place in her heart or her life. "Thank you so much, for everything." He set the gloves aside and took her hand. "Truly. I am so thankful for this evening. It's been wonderful." The card was sitting right there. He wasn't much for sentimentality, but he would cherish it forever, even if things didn't work out, even if the horrible things he'd done came to light. "The gloves are absolutely perfect and the card is just..." He nodded, swallowing back everything he wanted to tell her. *I love you.* "It's perfect, too. You have such a way with words."

She smiled sheepishly. "I have a fair amount of experience with writing you notes and letters."

"I don't ever remember you writing to me."

She downed the last of the wine in her glass and refilled it, topping off his as well. "After that Christmas you stayed with my family, I had a hard time. Writing to you was my outlet."

"A hard time?" What in the world was she talking about?

She shrugged. "I just couldn't stop thinking about you. A lot of it was just wondering if you'd said no when I kissed you because you didn't like me. It had definitely occurred to me that you might have used Adam as an excuse."

Could she really think that? After all this time? "He wasn't an excuse. I was completely honest with you, Anna. If it hadn't been for Adam, I would've kissed you all night long. Your Dartmouth sweatshirt would've been off in a heartbeat."

She dropped her chin and grinned. "Really?"

"Yes. Really." Just thinking about it filled him

with equal measures of regret and gratitude. At least he'd gotten a second chance, but had he unwittingly thrown it away?

"So anyway, I wrote you letters. A lot of letters."

He narrowed his gaze. "But I never heard from you at all."

"I never mailed them. I kept them in a box. I threw them away right before I graduated from college. At that point, it felt pretty silly to still be pining for you, and I had a boyfriend. Although he didn't last for long."

"Why didn't you send them after my friendship with Adam went south?"

"You can't be serious. Didn't you hate my entire family at that point?"

He had to think hard about that. "I definitely told myself I hated all of you, but I never truly felt that way about you. Or your mom. You were both so kind to me."

"Would you have actually read them?"

He had to be honest. "Probably not. I was insanely angry those first few years. I probably would've just thrown them away." If only he could have thrown away that anger instead, he wouldn't be in this position right now. If only things with Adam hadn't ended the way they had. "Can you tell me what they said?"

Her face flushed with bright red. "You would ask that, wouldn't you?"

"I'm curious."

"Of course you are. They were all about you. Who doesn't want to hear about a bunch of love letters someone wrote about them?"

"Just tell me one thing." His curiosity was getting the better of him. It was difficult not to be fascinated by the idea of someone being that preoccupied with him. The thought of Anna feeling that way was nothing short of awe inspiring.

She laughed quietly and walked her fingers across the table until she took his hand. It covered his arm in goose bumps. What she could do with a single touch—it astounded him every time. "It depended on the day. If I was dealing with it okay, I would just write and tell you how much I missed you, but then I would write about normal things happening with me. If I was sad, then it was *a lot* about how much I missed you."

She cast her eyes aside as if she was trying to summon her courage. "And then there were the times when I was feeling lonely in other ways. That's when I wrote to you about what I wished would've happened that night."

Now he was really kicking himself for having turned her down that night. "Dammit. Really? And you threw those away? I'd pay just about anything to read that."

"How about if I just show you instead?"

Her eyes glinted with mischief, warming him from head to toe. Was he the luckiest man on earth? Because it sure felt that way. He not only needed her at that moment, he needed to have her as his forever. He couldn't imagine a moment without what they had together. That meant he needed to double his efforts to stop the Lang-Tel takeover. Then he could tell her he loved her. Then he could find a way to smooth things over with Adam. Then he could go to Tiffany's, buy her a big fat ring, and have what he knew he couldn't live without—Anna.

Eleven

Anna could no longer tiptoe around Adam. Hiding her relationship with Jacob had become ridiculous. His birthday had illustrated that they were moving in a good direction, but they were both clearly holding back. She'd sensed it all night from him, that there was something he was dying to say. Was it that he loved her? If those were the words he wanted to say, the only thing she could imagine stopping him was Adam. There was no other explanation.

Could she persuade Adam to set aside the feud? The more she thought about it, the more convinced she was that it could be fixed. If she could get her two favorite guys to bury the hatchet, everything in her life would be better.

Anna buzzed her assistant, Carrie. "Can you let me know when my brother is out of his meeting? I need to speak to him this morning."

"Sure thing, Ms. Langford. Anything else?"

Anything else. *Maybe get Adam's secretary to slip a shot of bourbon into his coffee cup.* "No, Carrie. Thank you."

Twenty minutes later, Anna got the call. "Mr. Langford can see you now."

She strode down the hall, feigning the confidence that wavered inside her. Her relationship with Adam had improved so much since he'd had his revelation about how hard their father's death had hit him, but she still had no idea how he would react to this news. Would he feel betrayed? Would he be angry? He'd be entitled to either reaction. She only knew that the time had come to finally own up to everything. It was her only chance to have Jacob, for real.

"Hey. What's up?" Adam asked, glancing up from his computer screen.

His upbeat and affable tone convinced her

she'd gotten the timing right. This was the morning for progress. "I was hoping to speak to you for a few minutes about something personal." She closed his office door behind her and took a seat opposite his desk.

He closed his laptop. "Of course. Is everything okay?"

"For the most part, everything is great, but it could be a lot better if I could just fix one thing."

"I'm listening."

"You and Jacob. I'd really like to see you two find a way to be civil to each other and stop the fighting. It's gone on for far too long."

He shook his head. "I thought you said this was personal. Sunny Side is not personal. And we agreed to table that."

"I'm not talking about that. I'm talking about me." Did she have the courage to say what had to come next? She had to do it. Now or never. "Me and Jacob. Together. Personally. Very personally."

His eyebrows drew together. "I don't understand."

"Me and Jacob. You know…"

"Working together?"

"Do I have to draw you a map, Adam? Jacob and I are involved. Romantically. Not business. Personal."

He reared back his head as if she'd just told him that the world was flat. "How in the hell did that happen? You can't be serious."

She took a deep breath to steel herself. She'd worried this might be his reaction. "I don't want you to be angry, but I went away with him. To his house upstate. About six weeks ago. That's where things started."

"Why in the world would you do that? Did he kidnap you?"

"Will you stop? That's just mean."

"Anna, this is making zero sense."

It was time to come clean and she knew it. "I went behind your back and met with the founder of Sunny Side."

"You what?" The fury in his eyes surfaced, just as it had the night they'd first discussed this.

She thrust her finger into the air. "Hold on, Adam. Let me finish. I was certain that I could convince you to come around if I had a better sense of the numbers. We need a strong financial upside these days, don't we?"

"That's not the point…"

"Just answer the question. Yes or no."

"Yes. We do."

"Okay then. That's what I was trying to do. And things just sort of happened between Jacob and me. And then it continued when we got back to the city. I want to see where it can go. We mesh together really well."

He twisted his face. "I don't even want to think about you two, meshing."

"That's not what I'm talking about and you know it." She scooted to the edge of her seat, folding her hands before her and resting her elbows on her knees. It was no coincidence that she looked as if she was praying. "I can't be with Jacob if you two are at odds. Family is too important. I can't be torn between the two. I understand that there's bad blood between you, but I need you and Jacob to sit down and work it out. Once and for all. It's been six years, Adam. You were both new in business. You both made mistakes."

He shook his head so vigorously that his normally perfect hair went astray. "If I made any mistakes, I made them because I was reacting to the things Jacob did. He could've ruined a multi-million-dollar idea."

"But he didn't."

"It doesn't matter. Jacob was willing to put our business venture at risk to prove a point. That told me that he was unreliable as a business partner."

"I just feel like this whole thing has gotten blown completely out of proportion. You used to be friends."

"So what are you hoping for? That I apologize and we start playing golf together? That's not going to happen."

"I'm not asking you to be best friends. I'm just asking for enough of a truce that you two can be in the same room without trying to kill each other. That's it. Although I'd be lying if I said I wouldn't be happy if you rekindled your friendship. That would be nice to see."

"You're deluded." He leaned forward in his chair, his eyes pleading with her. "He's scum,

Anna. I don't know what kind of line he fed you to get you into his bed, but I'm sure he was just trying to get back at me. You need to stop acting like a girl and walk away from him now, before you get hurt."

Anna was so offended on multiple levels that she wasn't even sure where to start. "Sometimes I think you just don't want me to be happy, Adam. You know, you and Melanie found a way. I don't see why you can't do one thing for me. For your sister."

"I'm not doing a damn thing to help my sister ruin her life. Believe me, some day you'll thank me." He opened up his laptop and stared at the screen.

She sat back, folded her arms across her chest, crossed her legs. She wagged her foot, brainstorming a new approach.

"Is there something else?" he asked.

"Nope." She shook her head with fierce determination. "I'm not leaving until we talk this out. I don't care if I have to sit here all day." She dug her phone out of her pocket. "I can do a remarkable amount of work sitting right here."

"Mr. Langford?" Adam's assistant's voice broke in over the intercom.

"Yes?"

"I'm so sorry to interrupt, but I have an urgent phone call from Samuel Haskins. He says it can't wait."

Anna grimaced. Sam Haskins had held a seat on the LangTel board of directors longer than anyone, even before Anna had been born. He was big on propriety and manners. He would never ask Adam to interrupt a meeting unless it were a life-or-death situation.

Adam picked up the phone. "Put the call through." He tapped his pen on the desk nervously, his forehead creasing. Right then she could see how much things weighed on him. It was the same sort of look her dad had when things at work were a bear. "Sam. What can I do for you?"

His sights darted to Anna after a few seconds. "So we were right all along."

What in the world could they be talking about? And did it have something to do with her? Why else would he look at her like that?

Adam nodded in agreement, but there was anger in his eyes. "Yes, of course. Whatever you think is the best course of action, but clearly we have to stop these guys. Now. I'll clear my schedule and we'll get on it right away. It's all hands on deck." He glanced at his watch. "Yes. I'll see you in an hour."

"What's going on?" she asked, trying to disguise the worry in her voice.

"Your boyfriend? Jacob? He's heading up a secret investment group. They're the ones buying up LangTel stock."

Her heart felt as if it didn't know whether to leap to action or keel over. "What are you talking about? That can't be right. I just saw him last night." *I've been seeing him every night.* This couldn't be right.

"Jacob Lin and a bunch of guys with a lot of money are preparing for a hostile takeover of LangTel. He's trying to destroy the company our father built, Anna. He's trying to destroy our family's livelihood."

"That can't be right." Her eyes darted all over his office, desperate for some sign that this was all a bad dream. "I'll go talk to him. Right now. This must be a mistake."

"It's not a mistake. Sam has the evidence. And if you were looking for proof that Jacob is scum, here it is."

Anna had never just shown up at Jacob's office. Not once. But here she was, standing in front of his desk after storming in, eyes wild, chest heaving, looking as though she was about to explode. What a relief that he'd put the bag from Tiffany's in his desk drawer. From the look on Anna's face, this was not the time to propose marriage.

"I'm going to have to call you back," he said into the phone, not waiting for a response before he hung up.

"Please tell me it's not true," she blurted, a distinct tone of panic in her voice.

Oh, no. His stomach sank as if he'd just swallowed an anvil. "Tell you what's not true?"

"You and your investment group, Jacob. Please tell me it's not true. Please tell me that Adam got some bad information. Because right now I feel like I'm going to be sick."

He closed his eyes and took a deep breath. His worst nightmare had just come true, but he couldn't lie to her. He'd already endured the guilt of not coming out with it in the first place, or even better, not starting the endeavor at all. "Please let me explain."

All color drained from her face. "Oh, my God. It *is* true." Her voice was fragile and delicate, as if she'd just been broken in half. It killed him to hear her sound like that and he was responsible. "I can't even believe this. Did you sleep with me just so you could get information about LangTel? Because Adam thinks you did. Has this whole thing been a big lie?"

"No. Of course not. How could you think that?" He stepped out from behind his desk, but she shunned him with a quick turn of her shoulder. The physical pain of her rejection resonated deep in his body, but he couldn't deny that he had it coming. "Adam knows about us?"

"Yes, Jacob. I went to him this morning to tell him. Do you know why?"

He shook his head. He couldn't imagine what had finally prompted her to share the thing they'd been hiding all this time.

"Because I hated the sneaking around. I wanted to give us a chance, a real chance. And now I find out that you were trying to destroy my family's company all along." The pain of the betrayal was clear as day on her face. She was shaking like a leaf.

He wanted to pull her into his snug embrace and make everything okay, fix the massive problem he'd created, except he couldn't. It wouldn't help anything. He'd messed up, in tragic fashion. "Will you please sit down so I can explain everything?"

"What could you possibly say that's going to make me feel any better?"

Again, she was right. "Look. I know now that I shouldn't have started this, but the reality is that I never in a million years imagined that you and I would become involved the way we have. That came completely out of left field."

"And it would've been so awkward to roll over in bed and whisper in my ear that you were trying to take over the company my dad built from nothing. That definitely would've put a damper on the sex, huh?"

Every word out of her mouth drove the knife in his heart a little deeper, but he didn't dare flinch. He deserved it all. "I went on the counter-offensive the morning after we first made love. That's what I was doing out in the garage before we left. I called my closest friend in the group to try to convince them to back off."

"So what happened? Why are you guys still trying to do this?"

"*We* aren't trying to do anything. They ousted me. Yesterday. They were tired of me pushing so hard to end the LangTel takeover."

"Does that mean you have no more pull with them? They're really just going to go ahead and do it without you?" She sighed and stared out the window. "This is getting worse by the minute."

"They say they're going to. I don't really have a way of knowing. Believe me, I've been racking my brain, trying to come up with a way to stop them."

Her jaw tensed. She shook her head. "What

was the plan, Jacob? Tell me the plan you had before I came along. If you want any chance of redeeming yourself in any way to me, tell me the plan."

"We planned to get enough stock to take over the board of directors and oust Adam as CEO."

"Oust Adam or oust the CEO?"

"Is there a difference?"

"In six months, there will be."

He almost wanted to laugh at his own short-sightedness. Of course. The board of directors was probably already trying to oust Adam. He hadn't thought about that. "Do they already have a successor picked?"

"You're looking at her."

It was as if all air in the room stopped moving. *Anna? CEO?* What had he done? "You?"

"Yes. Me. My dad gave his blessing before he died, but they had to put Adam in place first because that had always been the plan. I'm supposed to be the next LangTel CEO. It's my dream job. Not that it's going to happen now."

No. Good God, no. He'd set a plan in motion to

take away the dream job of the woman he loved. "Please let me try to find a way to fix this."

"You just said you've been trying to fix it for over a month. How are you going to magically make it happen now? And how am I supposed to trust you? We've been involved for weeks now, and the whole time you knew there were plans to dismantle my family's company. The company my dad spent decades building. You were best friends with my brother, Jacob. You stayed at our house. And now you want to destroy us?"

"I never wanted to destroy *you*. Never."

"Yeah, well, whether it was your intention or not, that's exactly what you're doing. You're destroying me and I can't sit around and watch it happen. Which is exactly why I never want to see you again. Ever." Her lip quivered. Was it because she was so angry? Or did it kill her to say those words as much as it killed him to hear them?

"I love you, Anna. I love you more than I ever thought it was possible to love someone. Please don't do this. I need you."

A single tear leaked from the corner of her

eye. "You love me? Why do you decide to tell me that now? When you have to save your own hide? Why couldn't you tell me last night when I was making you dinner for your birthday or singing you a song or..." Her eyes clamped shut. "Or when I was telling you that stupid story about the ridiculous letters. Do you have any idea how betrayed I feel right now?"

Again he was overwhelmed by his need to touch her, but everything in her body language said she would absolutely kill him if he took another step closer. "You have the right to feel all of this. I made a huge mistake and I'm so sorry. I just want the chance to make it better."

"I'm sorry, Jacob. I can't give you another chance at anything. Ever."

"But what about my feelings for you? Does that mean nothing?"

She stood a little straighter and looked him square in the eye. "Actually, it would have meant everything to me if you hadn't betrayed me. Because I love you too and now I have to figure out a way to fall out of love with you."

She loves me. The full repercussions of his

one vengeful act came at him with full force. He was about to lose the one thing, the one person, he truly cared about—Anna. "Then don't do it. Give me the chance to make it right."

"I can't. You took my love and threw it away. And that means we're done."

Twelve

Optimism. Anna would've done nearly anything to cultivate a single optimistic thought as she stalked through the LangTel halls to her office. The satisfaction she'd once felt about working here was gone. LangTel was officially embroiled in a battle for survival, against a threat that was impossible to defeat because there was no real way to build a stronghold. No one knew who the mysterious big investor was, and as much digging as Adam and Anna did, they came up with virtually nothing.

The fact that Anna had slept with the enemy only made her life more miserable. Luckily,

Adam had remained discreet about that fact, but it had made Thanksgiving especially tense. She prayed he wouldn't say something about it to their mother. It was bad enough that Evelyn Langford had to know about the threat of take-over—LangTel was the bulk of her sizable nest egg, after all.

For the moment, Anna's days were spent jumping through hoops for the board of directors, which had gotten her exactly nowhere, as they were likewise all consumed with the threat of a takeover. It all added up to one thing—her dream job felt more out of reach than ever.

And then there was her personal life, which in many ways felt more like her personal death. Having gone from the high of being with Jacob to the low of discovering what he'd been doing behind her back the entire time they were together had been far worse than jarring. It felt as if she'd been pushed off a cliff with no warning and most certainly nowhere soft to land.

Anna's assistant, Carrie, filed into her office with a cup of coffee. "Is there anything else I can get you this morning, Ms. Langford?"

"No, thank you." Anna settled in at her desk for the ten minutes of her day she actually looked forward to—reading the newspaper. At this point, she clung to the little things that made her happy. There weren't many.

"Oh, before I forget, Ms. Louis was looking for you this morning."

Anna glanced at her watch. "Can you buzz her and let her know that now is a good time?"

"Certainly." Carrie closed the door quietly behind her.

Anna unfolded the business section and was immediately sickened by the headline beneath the fold. Sunny Side had sold. To a rival telecom, no less.

She quickly scanned the article, her heart pounding, half out of shock and the other half out of anger. Somewhere in there was sadness, but she hadn't given in to that yet. It said that the sale was orchestrated by Jacob. So much for the big delay on their patent application. Was that another of his lies? Carefully crafted to lure her in? To what end, she did not know—seek revenge on Adam, get inside information on Lang-

Tel. Jacob had everything to gain and she'd had everything to lose. She simply hadn't known it because she'd trusted him—with business, with her heart and her body. *Bastard.* Just when he couldn't have possibly betrayed her in any worse a fashion, he had to go and twist the knife in her back. First he'd tried to destroy her family, then he yanked away her most promising business deal.

So that was it. Jacob really had moved on, in every way imaginable. The thought made tears sting her eyes, but she had to face the truth. There hadn't been so much as a peep from Jacob since they'd broken up. Not a single word. She'd spent nights wide awake, wondering why it had all gone so wrong. Why was the perfect guy also the one who most hated her family? Why was he the man who had so easily betrayed her? It felt like some cruel joke, a tragic twist of fate.

And Jacob? He apparently wasn't quite so torn up by what had happened, moving ahead with the Sunny Side deal. Nope. He'd gone right back to work, making his millions. Perfect.

Her eyes drifted to the picture accompanying

the headline. Jacob had that smile on his face, the one he wasn't quick to share, the one you had to coax out of him because he played everything so close to the vest. She missed that smile so much that it made her ache. And it was a longing for more than just him, it was a longing for the way she'd been with him—happy. It was also a longing for the possibilities of "us." Between her dad's illness, death and the company's troubles, the future had seemed bleak and uncertain for over a year. The notion of "us" had lifted her out of that state, but it hadn't lasted long.

Holly rapped on her office door. "Carrie said you have a minute."

Anna shuffled the newspaper aside and collected herself. "Yes. Of course. What's up?"

"I wanted to ask if you can sit in on my meeting tomorrow morning. Everybody seems to react more favorably to bad news when you're in the room, and there's a lot of bad news." Holly sidled in and plopped a muffin down on Anna's desk. "Here. I brought you some breakfast so you can't say no."

"Is that blueberry?" Anna scrunched her nose. The aroma had overtaken her office with an artificial, off-putting smell.

"Yes. Isn't it your favorite?"

Anna shook her head. "Usually. I guess I'm not very hungry this morning. Thank you, though. I appreciate it."

"Let me get this out of your way then." Holly reached for the offending pastry and marched it out of Anna's office. She returned seconds later. "Are you feeling okay today? You look a bit pale."

Anna hadn't been feeling well at all—tired and blah. Probably a bug of some sort. December was right about time for the first cold of the season. "I'm okay. Just a little run-down."

"Yeah, I hear that. I have the worst PMS right now."

PMS. A thought flashed through Anna's mind—when was the last time she'd had her period? Miami? That was two months ago. "I know how that goes."

"So you're in on this meeting? Please say yes." Holly smiled and batted her lashes.

"Sure thing," Anna agreed, now distracted by the new direction in which her malaise seemed to be pointing.

Holly left and Anna immediately pulled up the period tracker app on her phone. The notification was right in front of her seconds later. Forty-two days late.

"I'm never late," she muttered to herself, her brain slowly catching up. She pinched the bridge of her nose. *No. There's no way.*

She shook her head and dismissed it as silly. She couldn't be that. She couldn't be pregnant. It had to be stress. She hadn't just been under a lot of it, she'd been buried in it. Sucking in a deep breath, she ushered foolish thoughts out of her head and got to work.

A half hour later, her stomach rumbled and growled. The muffin might have been disgusting smelling, but she probably should've eaten it. She rolled her chair over to the office credenza where Carrie had stashed some snacks. A protein bar seemed like a good idea, but the moment she tore open the package and got a whiff of chocolate and peanut butter, her stomach lurched again.

It has to be the stomach flu. I should go home.

She packed up her laptop, put on her coat, and stepped out of her office. "You know, Carrie, I think I'm coming down with something. I'm going to work from home for the rest of the day, but it'd be great if you could run interference for me, at least a little. Just tell people to send me an email if they need me."

"And Mr. Langford? What do you want me to tell him if he asks?" Carrie cringed. Adam had bitten her head off last week. It was hard to blame him at this point.

"You're welcome to tell him I'm sick." No use sugarcoating it.

One of the company drivers took Anna back to her apartment, but she asked him to stop by the pharmacy on the way there. She dashed in, grabbed some pain reliever and seltzer. The line at the register was long, which only gave her more time to think about the improbable. Was she? The doctor had told her it was a virtual impossibility. Virtual. That didn't mean an absolute zero.

She turned back for a pregnancy test, admonishing herself for giving in to these ridiculous thoughts. As if she could be pregnant by her brother's biggest enemy, the man who'd started the war on her family's corporation. The entire idea was ludicrous.

When she got home, she whipped off her coat. Sitting in the car thinking about it had only made her that much more eager to put the idea to rest so she could curl up on the couch, turn on an old movie and slip into a vegetative state.

The instructions seemed simple enough—pee on the stick and wait. She did exactly that, studying the clock on her phone until the five minutes were up. Time to check.

Two blue lines.

She scrambled for the instructions, taking several moments before it sank in that she was reading the Spanish directions. She ruffled the paper to the other side. "Two blue lines, two blue lines," she mumbled, scanning the page. Two blue lines. Pregnant.

Oh, no no no.

The room felt like it was spinning, while her head traveled in the opposite direction and twice as fast. Pregnant? *I can't be.* She stared at the lines, but they only darkened the longer she looked at them, as if they were defying her to question the results. She consulted the directions again. *A false negative is far more likely than a false positive.*

What do I do? Who do I tell? Definitely not her mother. Her mother would freak out, and Anna was ready to freak out enough for a dozen people. She couldn't call Melanie. She loved Melanie, but she would blab to Adam and that would be bad. Very, very bad. The only answer was Holly. Holly was her biggest ally at LangTel, and if she were being honest, the only female she ever did anything fun with, like going out for drinks.

Holly's phone seemed to ring for an eternity. "Anna? You're calling me from your cell? Why didn't you just walk down to my office?"

"I'm at home. Can you talk without anyone hearing?"

"Two secs. Let me close my office door." There was a rustle on the other end of the line. "Okay, talk. Wait. Did you hear from you-know-who?"

"No." Anna rubbed her head. Good thing she'd bought that pain reliever. "I'm pregnant." No reply came from the other end of the line. "Holly? Are you there?"

"I just saw you two hours ago. What in the heck happened after I threw away the blueberry muffin?"

"It wasn't until you said that thing about PMS that I realized I'd completely skipped my period. So I came home and took a pregnancy test."

"Why didn't you tell me? I could've come with you."

"Because I was sure it was a stupid idea, that's why." It was worse than stupid. If she hadn't done it, she could've been going about her normal miserable day. Now she had to go about her pregnant miserable day.

"Do you know who the father is?"

"You can't be serious."

"You weren't together for much more than six

weeks. How many times could you possibly have had sex?"

Anna nearly snorted at the question. *You have no idea.* She and Jacob had been like rabbits. There was no escaping their physical attraction. It had a life force all its own. It had been made even more carefree by the knowledge that she couldn't get pregnant. Or so she thought. "Let's just say that he has a very short recovery time."

"No wonder you were so bummed out to break up with him."

Anna sighed. She had indeed been sad to break up with him, although sex wasn't the reason. She'd fallen in love with the big jerk. "He's probably going to be the reason LangTel will go down the tubes. I couldn't exactly look beyond that." She could never forgive him for that. He not only knew *exactly* what her family meant to her, he'd known it all along.

"No, I suppose not."

"So what do I do?" Anna hadn't even thought beyond this phone call. Making plans was not in her skill set at the moment.

"You have to tell Jacob."

"What am I supposed to do? Just waltz into his office and announce that I'm sorry that the last time I was there I had to tell him what a bastard he is, and by the way, I'm pregnant with your baby?"

"Think of it this way. It'll be ten times more awkward when you run into him on the street a year from now and have to explain where you got your little Asian baby."

A year from now. She might as well have been talking about the abominable snowman. Nothing seemed real anymore, especially not the future. Perhaps that was because she'd grown immune to all of it. Holly had a point, too. There would eventually be a baby to explain, to everyone. There'd be a baby bump before that. "I have to tell my family, too, don't I?"

"At some point, yes. Nothing makes Christmas morning more uncomfortable than a baby nobody knew about."

Anna laughed quietly. At last she had Holly around to lighten the mood. "You know what's ridiculous about this situation? I should be happy right now. I should be jumping up and down in the streets. I really want to have a baby. You know, I went to a fertility doctor about it after my dad passed away."

"Oh, honey. You did?"

"That's when they told me that I had so much scar tissue from my appendectomy that it was impossible to conceive until I had it fixed. I never had a chance to have the surgery."

"This is a miracle baby, Anna. I'm not exactly the sentimental type, but think about that. That's pretty special. Maybe this was meant to be. For whatever reason, the universe decided that you need this baby."

Tears sprouted in her eyes, just right out of nowhere. A miracle baby. "I don't know what to think anymore, honestly, but maybe there is a reason this happened."

"So when are you going to tell Jacob?"

"Can't I wait until after I go to the doctor? Maybe wait until the end of the first trimester just in case something goes wrong? The doctor had said the scar tissue could make carrying a pregnancy difficult."

"You have to tell Jacob, honey. No two ways

about that. He deserves to know and he deserves to know now. Every bad thing he did in the past doesn't change the fact that you and he made a child."

Thirteen

Jacob was drowning in the dead quiet of his apartment, but he didn't have the energy to go into the office. Life without Anna wasn't getting any easier. If anything, it was getting harder.

He sat back in his office chair, rubbing at his stiff neck, feeling sore and achy. He'd been working out too much, not sleeping at all, and eating too little. Self-inflicted discomfort seemed only fitting considering the damage he'd done.

It'd been two weeks now, and each day felt as if it stretched on for eternity, a never-ending dirge of meetings and deals and money. He'd once lived on the adrenaline of it. Now it all felt empty. Every night before he went to bed, he looked at the engagement ring he'd bought for Anna. All of his pain, both physical and emotional, served as a reminder of what he was still holding out hope for—that he would stop the LangTel takeover and win her back.

Jacob's phone vibrated on his desk. Did he even bother to look? Just another person wanting something from him, most likely, but he had to force himself to check. When he did, he stared at his phone in utter astonishment. *Anna.*

His heart did a double take, jerking into high gear. Why was she calling? Was it because of the Sunny Side deal? He didn't want to pin his hopes on anything, but he really hoped she was calling for some other, more personal reason. "Hey," he said, fumbling with the phone. Was that really the best he could come up with? He sounded like a teenaged boy.

"Hey," she replied. Her voice was sweet, but distressed, echoing in his mind throughout the most awkward silence Jacob had ever endured.

"How are you?" he asked, deciding the course of polite conversation was the only one to take at this time. He wasn't about to be defensive with her. Everything bad and ugly had already been said.

"I've been better. I need to talk to you and we probably shouldn't do it over the phone. In fact, I know we shouldn't."

"Okay. Do you want to give me a hint?" Honestly, even if she wanted to come over and yell at him some more, he would've agreed. He would've served refreshments. Anything to see her. Even if it would be painful. He was already hurting more than he could've ever imagined.

"Jacob, I just need to talk to you, okay? I can't bring myself to say it over the phone."

His heart went back to acting as if it didn't know what sort of speed was advised. Had she decided she could forgive him? Could he really be that lucky? And how long would it last if he was? There was still one indisputable fact— somewhere in the world, a very big shark was circling LangTel, and Jacob had dumped the blood into the water. If she lost her dream job because of him, there would be no coming back from that. "Yes. Of course. I'll come to you. Are you at the office?"

"Home."

He frowned. Anna never missed work. Ever. Had she left her job? Another big blow-up with Adam? Neither of those things made sense. She'd made it clear this was between them. Maybe she really was ready to reconcile. Maybe she felt as he did, that the other things between them, although messy, didn't usurp feelings. "I'm leaving right now."

The entire car ride was a lesson in patience, his curiosity killing him and his hopes refusing to be tempered, however much he wanted them to go away. He couldn't help it. He hoped she'd reconsidered.

Anna had left word with the doorman and Jacob took the elevator up to her floor, walking double-time down the hall to her apartment.

"Hi," she said when she opened the door.

The vision of Anna hit him the way an avalanche throws a mountain of snow down to the foothills. Her cheeks were blanched and her eyes pink and puffy. She'd been crying. Whatever this was, it was bad. He filed in to her kitchen, immediately plunged back into the familiar comfort of being with Anna, the one that made him feel as though he never wanted to be anywhere else, even when she was standing before him with her arms crossed, leaving a barrier between them.

"I don't want to make this any more of a big deal than it already is," she said, sniffling. "I'm pregnant and you're the only person who can be the father."

"Pregnant?" He remained calm on the outside, but his mind raced so fast he didn't know which way was up. His brain was a jumble of contradictory thoughts. A baby?

"Yes, Jacob. Pregnant."

Was this some sort of trick? "But I thought you couldn't get pregnant."

"I thought the same thing. The doctor had said it was virtually impossible for me to conceive."

"Virtually? So not completely impossible? Because you told me it was flat-out impossible."

"Virtually, completely. Does it really make that big of a difference?" She rolled her eyes. "Maybe you have superhero sperm. I don't know. Don't assume this is my fault. And remember, we were both there. It's not like I went and did this on my own."

Superhero sperm. His male ego wasn't about to argue that point. He started to say something else, to continue the argument, but one thing that had made him successful in business was his ability to accept facts and deal with problems, rather than burying his head in the sand. A pregnancy—a baby. That was a fact.

He'd told himself he would never have children. Not after the way his parents raised him— moving him from boarding school to boarding school, depending on his father's opinion of whether or not Jacob was being challenged enough with his studies. His dad pushed and pushed. There was no other speed and there was no nurturing any skills beyond academic, except for maybe the years he'd been forced to play classical piano when what he'd really wanted to learn was how to play guitar.

Was it even in his DNA to be loving and caring the way a dad should be? His father had given him a mind for business and that was about it. Such was the legacy of Henry Lin—mold your child in your image and tell him hundreds of times that you expect him to stay that way. Jacob had done it for the most part. After all, he was exceptional at doing exactly what his father did—making money. He had homes and cars and bank accounts to prove it. He merely didn't want to repeat his father's mistake, which had been becoming a dad in the first place.

"Jacob? Are you even listening to me? Are you going to say something?" Anna asked.

He shook his head and ran his hand through his hair. "I'm sorry. It's just that I'd never thought I would ever become a dad. This is just a lot to deal with at one time."

Anna's jaw dropped. "This is a lot for *you* to deal with? Why don't you ask the person who had to pee on a plastic stick how she's feeling about all of this?" She wrapped her sweater around her tightly. "I should've known better than to think that you would even care about this. You care about money and your pride and your stupid motorcycles and that's about it. Obviously the man who decided it was perfectly fine to destroy my family wouldn't care at all about the fact that he was going to be a dad. Goodbye, Jacob. Have a nice life. Don't make me call the doorman and tell him to come up here." She whipped around and rushed out of the room.

He chased her down the hall, grabbing her arm just outside her bedroom door. "Anna, stop."

She turned, not making eye contact, her chest heaving. "Just let me go, Jacob. Just let me go."

Her words, broken and desperate, gnawed at his heart. How could he let her go? He didn't want to. He'd spent the last several weeks missing her, desperately. "I'm sorry. Truly." The words about to roll off his tongue next, the ones about wanting to embrace her, wanting closeness with her just wouldn't come out. His feelings about Anna hadn't changed since the breakup, but being near her was a powerful reminder of how badly losing her had hurt in the first place. "Tell me what I can do."

She sucked in a deep breath. "I don't need you to do anything, okay? I'm a grown woman and

I can handle this on my own. Obviously this is more than you're equipped to deal with, so don't worry about it. I'll have plenty of support from my family. The baby and I will be fine."

A vision materialized—Anna and a baby. *The* baby. *Their* baby. Could he go on with his everyday life knowing they were out there doing the same without him? And what kind of man would that make him? Not only no better than his father, he would be far worse. "No, Anna. You're not going to handle this on your own. I will help you with whatever you and the baby need."

"I don't want you to do this out of some sense of obligation. That's not what I want."

"Well, of course that's part of it. How can it not be? This is just as much my responsibility as it is yours. Just because you're carrying the child doesn't mean that I don't need to share the burden equally."

"Burden? Is that how you see this? Because if you're going to use words like that, I can't even have you around. I need support. My entire life has fallen apart in the last year. I lost my dad,

I've probably lost my dream job, and don't forget that my family's corporation is in serious danger of being dismantled, in large part, thanks to you. How is this even going to work, Jacob? How will we ever find a happy medium when my family hates you and you hate them right back?"

When she had the nerve to be so blatant with their circumstances, it certainly did seem as though they were screwed. The weeks apart of wanting her back hadn't changed any of it. "I don't hate your family, Anna. Your brother and your family are not the same thing. I can see that much. I had very strong feelings for you. Much stronger than I ever anticipated. I told you I was in love with you and I meant it. That didn't go away."

"But it did go away. You lied to me."

"I kept the truth from you. To protect you. I couldn't put you in the middle of the mess I'd made. I don't know why you can't see that."

"I don't want to argue semantics. I'm just telling you how I feel. That hasn't changed."

"Okay. Fine. I get it. Regardless, I'm not going to walk away from you and this baby." Had he really just said that? A baby. It was far too sur-real. "I'm all-in."

"You do realize this isn't a card game. We're not placing bets."

"Of course I know that. I'm not an idiot."

"And I need to know that you're sure. This is an all-or-nothing proposition. You don't get to change your mind later."

"I'm not going to change my mind."

"We don't even know what's going to happen. The doctor didn't just tell me that I couldn't con-ceive, he told me it would be nearly impossible for me to carry a pregnancy to term."

How much more harsh reality could there be between them? Not much. "I understand. It doesn't change the fact that I'm half of this and that means I will participate and be there for whatever you need."

She sighed deeply and rewrapped her sweater around her waist, binding it to her body tightly. It was hard to believe there was a tiny person growing inside her—one half her, one half him.

"Just so we're clear, this does not mean we're back together," she said resolutely. "We'll have to work out the specifics when the time comes, but this partnership is about having a baby and that's it."

He fought the exasperated breath that wanted to leak out of him. He deserved this, the universe's way of reminding him that every action brought a reaction. He'd done the wrong thing, and atoning for that apparently came in the form of partnering with the woman he loved while under direct orders that there would be no reconciliation. "Clearly, you're calling the shots here."

She looked down at the floor, and when her eyes returned to his, he could see exactly how scared she was. It brought back, with a vengeance, the all-too-familiar ache for her. "Well, if you want to be involved, you can start by coming with me to my first doctor's appointment. Thursday. Ten a.m."

Jacob had a huge meeting scheduled that morning—a deal he'd been working on for months. "Of course. I'll be there."

Fourteen

Hospitals. One step inside and Anna was reminded of her dad—the months he spent fighting, in and out of the cancer ward, receiving treatments that they'd pinned so much hope on, only to ultimately lose. She wasn't sure she could deal with another loss like that, and she was already so attached to the idea of the baby.

"We're going up to the sixth floor." Anna pointed to the bank of elevator doors straight ahead. When the doctors realized who Anna was and the serious straits she was in from the beginning, they'd moved her first prenatal appointment to the specialist's office at the hospital. They wanted her to see a physician well-acquainted with high-risk pregnancies. Having that extra care was a comfort, but she really wished she didn't need it at all.

Jacob held the elevator door for her, being as gentlemanly as could be. She shoved her hands into her coat pockets. How she would've loved to be able to take his hand, squeeze it, have a true partner in all of this. But she didn't. He was the obligated dad. It had taken the pregnancy announcement to bring him back into her life. She hadn't heard a word from him after they broke up. Of the many things she had to get past, that now felt like the most difficult.

They reached their floor and stepped out into a quiet hall. There were several clinics along the corridor, theirs a few doors down. A woman at the reception desk welcomed them and had them take a seat.

A man across from them opened a breakfast sandwich of some sort, even when there was a very clear sign inches from his head saying there was no food or drink allowed. Anna loved eggs and bacon, but this morning the smell made her want to hide her head in a trash basket. Why wasn't the receptionist doing something about it? She was just sitting there, shuffling paper.

Anna turned into Jacob's arm, pressing her cheek and nose to the black wool of his coat, closing her eyes and drawing in one of the few scents she found appealing—woodsy and warm and surprisingly calming.

"You okay?" he asked, lowering his head to hers. When she looked up, their noses were inches apart.

She was caught in the fierce intensity of his dark eyes, which left her lips quivering. She would've done anything to be where they were weeks ago. Why did she have to have such strong feelings for him? Things would be so much easier if she didn't still want him. "It's the smell of his sandwich," she whispered.

Jacob stood and took Anna's hand, urging her to join him. "Come on." He marched over to the receptionist's desk. "Yes, excuse me. My wife is feeling a little queasy. I think she would feel more comfortable if we could be alone back in the examination room, if that's all right."

"Your wife?" Anna mumbled under her breath.

"The nurse will be out any moment now. It won't be much longer," the woman said.

"It's okay," Anna whispered. "You don't need to make a fuss."

"She's uncomfortable. You need to help me fix that." He cleared his throat.

The receptionist glared at him. "As I said, sir. One more moment."

He grasped Anna's hand. "I understand, but it's literally killing me to watch my pregnant wife suffer. So if you could please find us a place to get settled, that would be wonderful."

"Fine, Mr., uh…" She reached for a folder. "Mr. Langford."

Anna prepared for him to explode, but Jacob took it in stride.

"I'm Mr. Lin. She's Ms. Langford."

"Oh, yes. Of course." She picked up the phone. "Two seconds."

A nurse quickly emerged from the door next to reception and brought them back to a private room. "The doctor will want to speak to you and then do the pelvic exam. You can change into the gown after I take your vital signs." She took Anna's blood pressure and temperature, as well as her weight, then left them alone.

"You really didn't have to make a fuss about it, and I appreciate it, but please don't call me your wife," Anna said. There were enough gray areas. They didn't need more.

"Would you have preferred I identify you as the woman I impregnated? And don't forget it's my job to take care of you." Jacob unbuttoned his coat and put it on the hook, then took hers from her.

"It's your job to help me with the baby, when and if the time arrives."

"You are the vessel carrying the baby, and I don't like seeing you suffer, anyway. It's physically painful for me."

Remarks like that made her wonder if she'd made a mistake by telling him. The baby was not supposed to be a way back in for him, at least not into her heart. She had to protect herself from him as much as she could, however much they were already tied for a lifetime now. Even if the baby never arrived, it would be impossible to escape the fact that they had once shared this. And it would make it unthinkable to ever forget him.

She caught sight of the examination gown. "I need to change. So you need to step out into the hall."

"Anna. I've seen every inch of you. I could probably tell the doctor a few things. Don't worry. I won't stare." He sat down, pulling his phone out of his pocket, quickly reading something, and turning it facedown on his leg. "Too much."

"Uh, no. Close your eyes right now."

"Why?"

"Because I said so."

"Fine." He twisted his lips and did as he was asked.

She shucked her clothes and put on the gown in record time, then climbed up on to the exam table, covering her bare legs with the paper drape they had provided. "You can open your eyes now."

He crossed his legs and gave her a look that was far too familiar. "Next time, I'm looking."

"Next time you're standing in the hall. And you'd better be on the other side of the room during the exam."

A knock came at the door and a trim woman with long, curly red hair entered the room wearing a white lab coat. "Ms. Langford." She shook Anna's hand. "I'm Dr. Wright. It's nice to meet you." She turned to Jacob. "I take it this is Dad."

Jacob cleared his throat, seeming uncomfortable. "Jacob. Lin."

Dr. Wright wheeled over a rolling stool and scanned Anna's chart, nodding and humming. Lord only knew what she was thinking. She didn't show a reaction of any kind. Was that a good thing? A bad thing? After a few minutes, she closed the folder and stood. "All right, Ms. Langford. Let's have a look at you."

Anna lay back as the doctor took out the stirrups. Luckily, Jacob was following orders and had retreated to the far corner of the room. In all actuality, he'd created as much distance between them as possible. This was likely not a comfortable scenario for him, and she did have to admire him for not complaining or excusing himself.

Dr. Wright completed the exam and helped Anna to sit up. "Well, I'll be honest with you both. This is a tricky situation you've gotten yourselves into. I've seen the ultrasound images from your appointment with the fertility doctor. As to how you two got pregnant, I'm mystified. You must've been trying very hard."

Anna's face flushed with heat. Jacob snickered.

"Now, our hope is that this is a big, strong baby like Dad and that as he or she grows, the scar tissue has no choice but to give way. The worst case is that the baby gets stuck in a bad spot and the umbilical cord is squeezed or the baby simply can't grow."

Anna sat frozen. Dr. Wright dealt with dire situations every day, so it all came out of her mouth as if it wasn't a big deal. For Anna, this was a very big deal, and she was trying so hard to keep it together.

"Either way," Dr. Wright continued, "we'll have to watch you very, very carefully. You're most likely to lose the pregnancy early on. I'm guessing from your chart that you're almost eight weeks along, which is great. I need you to watch for spotting. Call us right away if that happens."

Anna sucked in a deep breath. "Okay."

Jacob stepped closer. "Dr. Wright, I'd like to know how many cases you've handled like Anna's and what the outcomes were. I want to make sure that Anna and the baby have the best of the best."

The doctor looked down her nose at Jacob. "I don't know the exact numbers, Mr. Lin. I assure you that I've handled many cases like yours, and I know what I'm doing. If you'd like to seek a second opinion, my nurse can provide you with some referrals."

Embarrassment flooded Anna. How could he do this? "No. Jacob, Dr. Wright has exceptional credentials."

"And I'd be a bad dad if I didn't ask about them."

"If you have concerns, Mr. Lin, you and I can talk about them some other time." Dr. Wright's voice was calm—almost soothing, but there was no mistaking the firm hand she was using with him. "We don't want Anna upset or experiencing any undue stress. It's not good for her or the baby."

"Oh. Okay." He nodded. "Good to know. No stress."

"That's probably the most important thing you can do, Anna. Avoid it at any cost. Jacob, you need to buffer her from it as much as possible. Sex can help, since it's such a good stress reliever."

Jacob coughed. "Did you hear that, honey?" he asked, wagging his eyebrows at her.

Anna pursed her lips. First he'd pulled the wife thing in the waiting room. Now this. "Is that really safe for the baby?"

"Actually, yes. The baby's so small right now." The doctor pulled a funny-looking instrument, like a tiny microphone, from a drawer near the exam room sink. "Let's see if we can find the baby's heartbeat."

Anna had read about hearing the heartbeat

with the fetal Doppler monitor. The notion both thrilled and terrified her.

"Just lie back," Dr. Wright said, lifting up Anna's exam gown to reveal her bare belly. She squirted some liquid on to her skin. "Just a bit of gel. It'll help pick up the sound."

A crackling sound like an old transistor radio broke out in the room. Jacob inched closer to Anna, bewildered. "We'll actually hear the baby's heartbeat?"

The doctor nodded, moving the instrument over Anna's stomach. "The heart forms and starts beating from a very early stage."

More static came from the small speaker the doctor held in her hand. Pops. Snaps. A rapid, watery sound rang out—likes waves at the beach on fast-forward. *Whoosh whoosh whoosh.* A smile spread across Dr. Wright's face. She nodded, consulting the instrument. "There's your baby."

Jacob held his breath. *Whoosh whoosh whoosh.* He'd never been so overtaken by shock and wonder, both at the same time. The miracle of the moment began to sink in, but it wasn't a weight.

Not as he'd worried it might be. The baby was not an idea or an abstract—the life that he and Anna had created, against all odds, was real. A tiny human, with a heart and everything. *Whoosh whoosh whoosh.* He'd never been so affected by a sound. That sound and the life force that created it needed him. Anna needed him. And he would not let either of them down.

Anna looked up at him, her eyes wide with astonishment. "Our baby," she muttered.

"It's absolutely incredible," he said, taking and gently squeezing her hand. Maybe it was the wrong thing to do, but he was acting on pure instinct. She didn't protest, which felt like such a gift. "It's so fast."

"It's a tiny heart, Mr. Lin. It doesn't know any other speed."

"And what does the baby look like right now? When can we see it?" *It?* That didn't sound right at all. "I mean him."

"Or her…" Anna added, smiling. It was the first truly light moment of the appointment or for that matter, since she'd told him she was pregnant. He was so grateful for it. Finally, some good news.

"Or her," Jacob agreed. "When can we see him or her?" He was no longer surprised by the excitement in his voice. It was impossible not to get caught up in the moment.

"We'll schedule an ultrasound for next week. I'd like to do some 3D imaging. For now, the baby looks like a peanut with a big forehead."

"Hmmm," Jacob said. Had his dad been this involved when his mother was pregnant with him? Had he gone to a single doctor's appointment? Jacob doubted it greatly. It was too bad—he'd missed out on so much. Jacob wouldn't have traded this experience for anything. It was only made better by the fact that he was with Anna. Now if he could only convince her to stop tabling romance and let him back into her heart.

The doctor put away the monitor and wiped off Anna's stomach.

"Where can I buy one of those?" Jacob asked. Being able to listen to the baby's heartbeat any time they wanted would be amazing. His mind drifted to thoughts of him and Anna in bed, listening to their baby's whoosh. Certainly their baby had an exceptional whoosh, far better than other babies' whooshes.

"There are inexpensive ones, but they don't work very well. The quality ones are in the neighborhood of six or seven hundred dollars."

"Oh yeah. We need one of those. Can your nurse order one for me?"

"That's a big expense for something you'll only use for another six months."

"And you think I really care about that," Jacob replied. "Because I don't."

Anna shook her head, grinning at him. "He doesn't care about that. At all."

Dr. Wright left after a reminder to watch for spotting, and a promise that they would all talk after the ultrasound. It was a scary, but exciting proposition, the thought of actually seeing the baby. He could only imagine how he would feel then. Everything that had just become so real would be even more so.

Walking down the hospital hall, riding on the elevator, through the lobby and back outside into the cold, gray December day, Jacob could hear that peculiar whooshing in his head. He and Anna and the baby were in the most precarious of situations, and he was determined to hold on to it with both hands. That wasn't at all the way he'd expected he would feel after today, but the heartbeat had changed everything.

Fifteen

"Are you doing okay over there?" Jacob asked as the limo sped along Lexington Avenue to Anna's apartment.

Anna wasn't okay. She wanted to be okay, but her mind kept dwelling on the medical issues. She looked out the window, entranced by the city passing her by, the people bustling along the sidewalks, in a rush that never ended. Had any of them received life-or-death news today? Probably. She wasn't so foolish to think she was the only person with problems.

"Anna." Jacob placed his hand on her shoulder.

"Talk to me. It's okay if you're upset after the appointment. It was a lot to take in. I understand."

She closed her eyes for a moment, trying not to fixate on his touch, which called to her, even through her winter coat. Being with him brought back a lot of wonderful feelings, but something tempered it. Could she count on him? For real? She turned back to him, fighting the tears that welled at the corners of her eyes. "Do you, Jacob? Do you really get it? Because our baby is inside me and you said yourself that you'd never planned on becoming a dad."

He nodded eagerly. "And I feel like a fool for even thinking it. I'm telling you, the second we heard the baby's heartbeat, everything changed. I get it. I do."

She sat back in the seat, picking at a spot on the leg of her pants. It was hard to look him in the eye—he was so upbeat and eager right now, but was that just the rush of the appointment? Would it wear off? She didn't have the luxury of worrying whether he would be there for her and the baby. "It felt different then for me, too. Except in some ways, it just made me more scared.

I'm going to be crushed if we lose this baby. Absolutely crushed. And every minute that goes by with this child growing inside of me, I'm going to change. I'm going to become more attached."

"Come here," he said, pulling her into his embrace. He rubbed her back as her head settled on his shoulder. "It's going to be okay. I promise."

Part of her wanted to be able to accept everything he'd said at face value, the way a child does when they're worried about monsters under the bed. He rubbed her back and anger bubbled inside her because she loved being like this with him. She wanted things back to the way they'd been before—before the world came crashing down, before he'd betrayed her, except this time, with the baby. Could she find a way to forgive him?

She wanted to let the bad things go, but one thing wouldn't stop nagging at her. If he had truly wanted her back after the breakup, why didn't he reach out? Why didn't he fight for her? It had taken the pregnancy announcement to bring him back into her life, but that didn't mean he actually wanted to stay. What would happen if she lost the baby? Would he walk away? Would the issues that came along with being with her be more than he wanted to deal with? "Don't promise that everything will be okay. No amount of money or planning or crossing our fingers is going to make everything fine. We have to wait and see what happens and that's going to kill me. It's going to be so hard."

"You have excellent medical care. You're in the best possible hands."

"Thanks a lot for raking my doctor over the coals. What in the hell were you thinking?" She pushed away from him and shook her head.

"I want the best for you and for the baby. You can't fault me for that. Someone has to ask the hard questions."

"I didn't pick a random doctor off the internet, you know. I swear. Sometimes you and Adam are so alike it's ridiculous. Neither one of you trusts me to do what's right."

"That's not true. I trust you implicitly, and I'm sure your brother trusts you, too. He's just gone through a particularly misguided phase since your father passed away."

"It almost sounds like you're defending him. Are you?" She narrowed her stare. It was the first nonvenomous thing that had come out of his mouth regarding Adam. "Because that would be truly weird."

"I'm only pointing out that Adam is a smart guy. He'd have to be an idiot not to see how amazing you are."

She rolled her eyes. "Lay it on thick, much?"

"Anna, come on. I'm just being honest. Can't we be honest with each other? After everything we've been through and with everything we're about to go through, I think it's only wise that we're truthful in everything."

Truthful? Was he really going to throw that at her now? "Ironic, coming from you."

He choked back the growl in his throat. "I was protecting you."

Protecting me. Really? "Tell yourself whatever you need to. That's not how it felt." The driver pulled up to the curb in front of Anna's building, then got out of the car to open her door. She couldn't even look back at Jacob to say goodbye. That would be too difficult when she was busy grappling with too many emotions. It would be so easy for him to look at her a certain way and she would be hopelessly drawn in, wanting to curl up into him and let him do exactly what he'd promised, the impossible—protect her. "I'll call you when they schedule the ultrasound."

Jacob was saddled with the most uneasy feeling he'd ever had. Anna and their baby were about to leave him. And she was upset. She shouldn't go upstairs and stew for hours. "Let me come in for a minute. We should talk."

"I'm tired of talking. And don't you need to get into the office?"

He was thankful he'd left his phone on vibrate. It'd been going crazy all through the appointment and during the car ride, but she didn't need to know that his business world might be falling apart while he was out of pocket. "You're more important right now."

She shook her head, seeming even more annoyed. "Fine."

They walked into the building and took the elevator upstairs. He liked feeling like this, almost as if they were a couple again, even if she was mad at him. What would it take for her to want him back? A lot of things, most likely—an absolute guarantee that LangTel was safe from a corporate takeover, a reconciliation with her brother.

"You really want to come in?" she asked once they arrived at her door. She had that icy tone in her voice, as if she were trying to freeze him out.

"I do." As they walked inside, he couldn't escape the feeling that this was only half right. He might be clueless about the notion of becoming a father, but he knew that they should be doing this together. If at all possible, this child should arrive with two loving parents, not a mother and a father fighting to remain civil. He didn't want to upset her, but perhaps it was time to just let her say her piece so they could finally more forward. "Anna, will you please tell me what I can do to make this better? Right now I feel like I'm stepping through a minefield."

She pursed her lips. "I'm supposed to stay calm."

"You're supposed to avoid stress, and walking

around with all of this anger welling up inside of you is not good. Just let it out. Let me have it."

"Right here? Right now?"

"No time like the present." He took off his coat and slung it over the back of a chair in the living room. He was ready for her to start yelling and he would sit there and take it until she got it all out. "Like I said, let me have it. Tell me every last thing."

"I don't want to rehash our problems. It's not like you don't already know how I feel. What bothers me more than anything is what happened after I broke up with you."

He furrowed his brow. "The Sunny Side deal? Mark found a buyer he wanted to work with. I never meant for that to hurt you."

"It's not that. It's that I never heard from you. You didn't fight it, you just accepted it and moved on. You didn't fight for me. That hurt more than anything."

Good God, if only she knew how much he had *not* moved on after she ended their relationship. He wasn't sure he could even own up to that. He'd never been so miserable, a shell of a man.

He didn't want to think of himself like that, the hopeless sap ruminating over his litany of mistakes, staring at the engagement ring he wasn't sure he'd ever have the chance to give her without her throwing it back in his face. "I did fight for you, it was just behind the scenes. I've been busting my hump to figure out who the secret LangTel investor is."

"See? That would have been good information to have, to at least know that you were trying."

"What kind of man would it make me if I came to you with half-filled promises? Trying and doing are two different things. After everything I did, you deserve better than that."

Anna sat down on the sofa, seeming deep in thought, but not saying a thing. Was he finally getting somewhere? He had to keep going.

"Anna, darling, I want you back. I think you know that. My feelings for you didn't go away when you said you were done with me. I still love you." He drew in a deep breath as he sensed his voice was about to break. Just thinking about today, about the baby, made his heart ache. "Now more than ever."

She raised her head slowly, her forehead creased with worry. "Because of the baby."

He took the seat beside her. "Some of it is, of course. There's no separating the two. But my love for you was there before you got pregnant, and it will be there tomorrow. It's not going anywhere. I'm not going anywhere."

"You're on a high right now from hearing the baby's heartbeat, from the excitement of what's new. How are you going to feel when we're forced to deal with my family? How are you going to feel if we lose the baby?"

Indeed, the road ahead was not getting any easier. He simply needed to know one thing. "Do you have feelings for me?"

She looked at him, scanning his face for what felt like a lifetime. "Part of me does. Part of me wants to punch you for what you did. It's hard for me to trust you. When I look back at our time together, all I can think about is everything you were keeping from me. That's hard to get past."

"Then maybe you need to try harder. I'll tell you I'm sorry until I'm blue in the face, but we had good times, too. Spectacular times. We had moments where I wasn't sure another person existed on the planet. Don't give up on our good memories. We can make more." He took her hand, relieved that she didn't fight the gesture. Body warmth traveled so easily between them— why couldn't everything else between them be so simple? Why couldn't things go back to the way they'd been at the beginning? So elemental. "I can't change the past. All I can do is try to build a future, but you hold the key. I can't do it without you."

She dropped her sights to their hands, joined. A tear fell onto her lap, darkening the fabric of her pants. "I need time to think. Today was a lot to deal with."

He nodded. Not that he had much choice, but he could accept that. He'd make do with a sliver of a chance. "I'll wait, but let me know if there's anything I can do to speed up the process."

"Right now, more than anything, I just need to know that you're not only in my corner, but that you're going to stay there."

"I am Anna. I am."

"I mean it, Jacob. For real."

He sucked in a deep breath of resolve. "I do, too. And I'll find a way to show you. I won't let you down."

Jacob rode the elevator to the lobby, deep in thought. So much had changed in the past few weeks. From the miserable depths of losing Anna, he had new hope. He couldn't afford to doubt the future—she was the one questioning what tomorrow held. He hated seeing that from her. She was the optimist, the sunniest part of his life.

He had to show her that there was more for them. It was the only way back into her heart. That meant showing her that he wasn't going anywhere.

When the doors slid open to the lobby, he was so immersed in his thoughts that he nearly flattened a man rushing on to the elevator.

"Sorry," the man said, holding up a blue Tiffany shopping bag. "Forgot the wedding anniversary yesterday. I'm in a hurry to get out of the doghouse."

"No problem," Jacob answered, turning and

watching the elevator doors slide closed. That flash of Tiffany blue was still there in his head.

If he wanted to show Anna that he wasn't going anywhere, he needed to make his overture. The question was when he would find the right moment.

Sixteen

Disbelief choked Jacob as he read the email the next morning—the missing piece of the puzzle, the information he'd been waiting on, sent by one of his informants. The identity of the high roller joining the War Chest was now known. Aiden Langford. And to think he'd woken up wondering when the right time would come to propose to Anna. That would need to be put off for at least another day.

He slumped back in the chair in his home office, sucking in a deep breath through his nose. His brain needed oxygen and fast. This was a huge problem and it had to be solved before it was too late. He knew that each Langford sibling owned 5 percent of the company. With that amount of stock in the mix, it would absolutely be feasible for Aiden to take down LangTel. And with everything Anna had once told him, Aiden had an axe to grind.

He wandered into his bedroom. Fixing the situation with Aiden wasn't a one-person job, and he couldn't go to Anna for help. It would expose her to far too much stress. He had to protect her and the baby. That left one person, the person he'd vowed to never trust again, especially when it came to business. He had to go to Adam.

He hopped in the shower and dressed quickly. It was time to find Adam, pronto, and there was no time for second-guessing what the outcome might be. The sooner they devised a plan to get Aiden under wraps, the better. Luckily, Adam was notorious for getting into the office absurdly early. Jacob asked his driver to take him to LangTel headquarters, sending Adam a text along the way.

We need to talk. Important. On my way to your office. Don't ask questions.

Adam's response came quickly. I'll tell security.

Jacob could only hope that Adam meant he was instructing security to let him *into* the building, not escort him out of it. He arrived at Lang-Tel in ten minutes and rushed into the lobby. A guard was indeed waiting for him, but only to issue a security badge and instruct him on which elevator to take for the executive floors.

Jacob's head was grinding, mulling over options, devising plans. Short of amassing a huge amount of money to buy Aiden out, how would they stop this? His heart pounded fiercely in his chest as he made his way down the hall to Adam's office.

Adam's assistant was waiting. "Mr. Lin?" She stepped out from behind her desk. "May I take your coat? Can I get you a coffee?"

Jacob mustered a polite smile and handed over his black wool coat. "No, thank you. I'm just fine."

"Mr. Langford is waiting for you."

"Actually, you can do one thing for me. Adam and I are discussing a surprise for his sister's birthday. If she comes by, make sure you don't let her in. Don't even let her know that I'm here." He raised his finger to his lips to encourage her compliance. He had to keep Anna away from this powder keg at any cost.

"Of course, Mr. Lin. Your secret is safe with me."

Jacob stood straighter and took extra-long strides into Adam's office. He tried to think of a time he'd had to swallow his pride any more than at this moment. He couldn't think of one, not even with his dad. Could he keep it together, stop himself from getting sidetracked by old problems?

Adam turned slowly in his massive leather executive chair like a villain in an action movie. "This is a surprise."

Jacob didn't wait for an invitation to sit, taking a seat opposite Adam's desk. "I'm as surprised as you are."

"Are you going to tell me why you're here or

are we going to play twenty questions?" Adam tapped a pen on the desk blotter.

"It's the War Chest."

"The gang of thugs you put together to take down the corporation my father built from the ground up? I know all about that."

It was so like Adam to bring up the most damning details. "The investment group I was kicked out of when I pushed them to stop because I didn't want a takeover to ruin my chances at a relationship with Anna."

Adam cleared his throat. "Don't get me started on Anna."

You have no idea. Adam was going to blow up when he found out that he and Anna were as involved as a man and woman could possibly be, even if the romantic side of things was fragile. "Please, Adam. I know I've done some things you aren't happy about. You can't say that you haven't done the same to me."

"I have a busy day ahead of me. Can you get to the point?"

"Your brother Aiden has joined the War Chest."

"What?" Fury blazed in Adam's eyes.

"With his percentage of stock in the mix, they can take over LangTel. Without much problem, I have to point out. You need to do something about this now."

"Oh, my God. Aiden." Adam's skin blanched, his eyes grew wide with disbelief. It was the first chink in Adam's armor that Jacob had ever seen. "He's been estranged from the family for years and it got worse when my dad got sick, but I never imagined he would go this far."

"Well, he has."

Adam's elbows dropped to his desk, and he pushed his hair back from his forehead. He twisted his lips. His stare narrowed. "Why didn't you take this to Anna? Was your breakup really that awful? I know she's not fun when she's mad."

Jacob had already covered up an awful lot with Anna, and the guilt from that might remain forever. He couldn't take the lies any further. "No, Adam. Anna is pregnant and I'm the father. I didn't want to tell her because stress could jeopardize the baby."

* * *

Anna walked through the quiet reception area on the executive floor, making her way to her office. She didn't normally get in so early, but she hadn't been able to sleep much. Perhaps the distraction of work would help clear her head before she ultimately returned to her worries about the baby and whether or not Jacob was really going to stand by her, no matter what.

"Good morning, Ms. Langford. Will you be joining Mr. Langford and Mr. Lin in their meeting?" her assistant, Carrie, asked as she took Anna's coat.

Anna froze in place. "Mr. Langford and Mr. Lin? Meeting? With each other? Here?"

"They're in Mr. Langford's office right now. I just assumed you knew." Her voice trailed off.

What in the world? Confused, she composed herself. "Oh, uh, yes. Yes, I'm joining them." Anna marched down the hall to her brother's office as if this had been the plan all along. A flurry of thoughts was turning her mind into a snow globe of speculation. Was this Jacob's way of fighting for her? Of showing her that he would take the worst of it? She could only hope that this meeting didn't end up with fists flying.

Adam's assistant bolted from her seat when Anna breezed past her and lunged for the doorknob to Adam's office. "Ms. Langford, I'm sorry. Mr. Langford is in a very important meeting…"

"So I heard." Anna marched into her brother's office. She wasn't about to wait to be invited in. Somebody could be dead.

She first saw Adam's response—surprise and shock. Jacob turned and showed a similar horror.

"Well, you're both still alive. So I guess that's good. Anybody want to tell me what's going on?" She planted her hand on her hip, assessing the situation. *What are these two up to?*

Jacob shifted in his seat. "We, uh, had a few things we needed to discuss."

"Right," Adam said, unconvincingly.

"You two can't stand to be in the same zip code. How about we try again?" She glanced over at Jacob, eager to glean from his facial expressions what was going on.

"Maybe it's time to finally change that," Adam interjected.

Now she had to make eye contact with Jacob. She tapped her foot on the floor. Something about this was off and she could see it on Jacob's face.

Adam blew out an exasperated breath. "This is stupid. Nobody's going to believe that you and I can actually talk to each other. Especially not Anna." He pointed at her. "Look. I know everything. I can't believe you're pregnant and you didn't tell me? Your own brother? And Jacob's the dad? I don't even know where to start with all of this. It's like a bad dream."

Jacob stood and grasped Anna's elbow. "I had to tell him. I'm sorry."

She closed her eyes and shook her head, drawing in a deep breath through her nose. The fact that he'd had the guts to come out with it certainly earned him a few points. "We had to tell him eventually. I just can't believe you came here to do this and that you didn't want me here at the same time."

"Well, that's not the only thing we're talking about," Adam said.

Jacob turned to Adam quickly, and even

though Anna couldn't see either of their faces head-on, she could tell they were having a conversation without words.

"Will somebody please just tell me what you're doing?" Anna asked. "I'm not leaving until one of you spills it."

"Well?" Adam asked, staring down Jacob. "Do you want to tell her, or should I?"

"Please. We have to stay calm. For the baby's sake," Jacob said, turning to her. "I found out who the War Chest brought in as their big investor. It's Aiden."

"What?" Anna asked. "Aiden? I don't understand."

Jacob looked at her thoughtfully, showing her his miraculous eyes. They were the only thing that calmed her in this unimaginable situation. He explained everything with Aiden as she struggled to keep up with the details. "It's very important that you don't get worked up about this. My first and only concern is for you and the baby."

Anna narrowed her focus on Adam.

"It's the one thing we didn't account for,"

Adam said flatly. "We're going to lose controlling interest in the company and I doubt there's much we can do about it. He's had a chip on his shoulder forever about LangTel, and you know how he feels about me in particular. Jacob and I were just strategizing on ways to raise the capital to fight this."

Anna sat down in the chair next to Jacob's. This was not the time for panic. There had to be a solution. "No. Adam, you have to reach out to him. Don't fight this with money. That's going to make things far worse. Send him an email. Tell him we know about it. But do it kindly. We don't want to scare him. Tell him that we want to talk, that we want to find out what would make him do this."

"How is that going to work?"

"You have any other bright ideas? He's our brother. If we do anything less than extend the olive branch, he'll never forgive us. Put yourself in his shoes."

"Maybe you should do it. He actually likes you." Adam's voice had an uncharacteristic wobble. Their father had left an awful lot on Adam's shoulders—the CEO position, now this. The root of the problem with Aiden was undoubtedly their father. He'd pitted the boys against each other from the very beginning.

"I think it will mean more from you, especially if you use a softer touch," she said. "He'll expect you to be all bravado, so don't do that. Be his brother."

"This is business. Do you really think that's advised? It sounds awfully girly."

Anna sat back in her chair and crossed her legs. "Then ask Jacob what he thinks."

Adam cocked both eyebrows at Jacob. Anna was amazed they'd managed this much without taking pot shots at each other.

"Anna's right," Jacob said, taking his seat next to her. "If your brother is feeling like he's on the outs with your family, it's going to take a softer approach. If you try to steamroller him, he'll steamroller you right back. Except he can flatten you with this one, Adam. Completely."

Adam looked as befuddled as Anna had ever seen him. "That's a surprising answer coming from you, Mr. Number Cruncher."

"I know exactly what it feels like to be on the outs with the Langford family. It's not a fun place to be."

Anna swallowed, hard. She couldn't argue that point. The good news was that as of now, Adam and Jacob had to be going on at least twenty minutes of being in the same room and everyone was still living and breathing.

Adam visibly tensed. "Okay. I'll do it. I'll play the nice guy and reach out to him." He went to his laptop and started typing. After a few keystrokes, he looked up at the two of them. "Are we done? I have work to do. I'll let you know when I hear back from Aiden."

Jacob cleared his throat and stood up. "Actually, there's one more thing."

"What?" Adam pushed back from his desk and crossed his arms.

"I need you to know that I love your sister more than anyone or anything on this entire planet. And I'm hoping that she and I can find a way to work things out, but we have some obstacles to get past and I want to get rid of one of them right now. You and I need to drop the fighting. It's stupid, and frankly, I have more important things to worry about."

"Do you really think it's as simple as that?" Adam retorted. "We decide to forget it? I can't believe that you, of all people, would think that you could just come in here and declare a truce and make it all go away. It's far more complicated than that."

"Actually, Adam, it's not. It's really very simple. Do we love Anna more than we hate each other?"

A puff of astonished air left Anna's lips. Six years of feuding and Jacob had boiled it down to one question.

"I know what my answer is," Jacob continued. "I love her far more than I ever hated you, which should tell you just how much I love her. Because I really, really hated you."

Adam sat back in his chair, his jaw slack. He was clearly letting this tumble around in his head, and they had to let him process it. "Wow. I guess you really can make it that simple." He looked at Anna, seeming to get a little choked up. "Anna Banana, I definitely love you more than I hate him. I don't know what I would've done during the last year without you."

"Then let's bury the hatchet, Adam. Please," Jacob added.

"If it will make Anna happy, I will give up the fight."

For the first time in a long time, she felt as if she could breathe without worry. "It would make me insanely happy. There's enough trouble going around for all of us." She stood and walked over to her brother to give him a hug. Relief washed over her.

"I can't believe I'm going to be an uncle," Adam muttered into her ear, holding her close, not letting go.

It would've been so nice to agree that indeed he would, but they weren't out of the woods. "Fingers crossed that everything goes okay."

"Anything you need at all," Adam said, stepping back, but still holding on to her shoulders. "Just let me know."

"Of course. I will."

"As for you," Adam said, reaching out his hand

to shake Jacob's. "I didn't really think this day would come. It'll be good to put it behind us."

Jacob smiled. "It's long overdue."

Anna led the way out of Adam's office. "That's not quite how I expected to start my day," Anna muttered to Jacob in the hall. One enormous problem had been resolved, even if another—Aiden—had cropped up.

"Can we talk?" he asked.

Her staff and coworkers were already milling about. The sight of Jacob Lin in the office was prompting hushed voices and sideways glances. "Of course, but not here. My office." She marched ahead, Jacob in her wake. They passed Holly when they rounded the corner to Anna's office. Holly bugged her eyes, but kept her mouth shut. Anna would have to fill her in later. She closed the door behind them, unsure where to start, only that she knew he deserved an awful lot of credit. "That must've been so hard for you to swallow your pride with Adam. I'm just floored that you would do that for me."

"It was for *us*, Anna. It had to end."

She found herself hopelessly drawn to him—

his voice, his presence. When he stripped away her defenses, her reasons for being mad or doubtful, he could have whatever he wanted. She looked up at him, peering into his penetrating eyes, the ones that left her undone. She'd asked him to fight for her, and he'd done exactly that. Big time. "I really admire you for it. I don't know what else to say, other than thank you. I know that couldn't have been easy."

"It wasn't, but I don't care about what's easy anymore. I care about getting you back."

Tingles raced over her skin, her breath caught in her chest. That rumble in his voice was there, the one that made her knees threaten to buckle. "Now what?"

"Have dinner with me tonight. My place."

He'd convinced Adam to let bygones be bygones. Could she do the same? Was she ready for this? Because she was certain that if she wound up in his apartment again, she was going to end up in his bed. Was that the logical next step? If it was, she knew very well that it led to a place where it was nearly impossible to be angry with him. Maybe that was for the best—finally just give in to what she wanted, finally just trust that this was the way things were meant to be. "I'd love to."

His smile was warm and immediate. "Good."

He cupped her shoulder gently and leaned in for a kiss—Anna nearly had a heart attack, her pulse erratic and frantic. She closed her eyes, her lips waiting for the reward, and then it arrived, square on her cheek.

She might've been disappointed if it wasn't so sweet, so warm and comforting, telling her that he was still letting her dictate their speed, even after he'd just put on a commanding performance. "Playing it safe?" She couldn't hide her smile. The ways in which he'd figured her out were uncanny.

"Baby steps. Literally." He placed his hand on her stomach gingerly. She felt his hesitation radiate from his core—he was holding back, employing restraint. "I'll see you tonight."

Seventeen

Jacob hadn't even made it down to the lobby before he had a text from Anna. He did a double take when he saw the message.

Don't leave. I'm spotting.

Was this really happening? Just when everything was finally going well? On my way up. What happened?

He stayed put on the elevator when it dropped people at the lobby, having to wait for what felt like an eternity as a new load of people boarded. It was just before nine, everyone on their way to work, which meant that nearly every button, for every floor, was pressed.

He took a deep breath. *Stay calm.* His heart wasn't cooperating at all, nor was his stomach. Everything in his body was on edge. Why now? Why this?

Anna sent a reply. Went to the bathroom and saw the blood.

Good God. Just when things were getting better. Don't worry. Be there soon.

He sent a text to his driver, instructing him to be ready to get them to the hospital as quickly as possible. Jacob would have to wait until he got somewhere private to call Dr. Wright's office. He couldn't announce in a crowded elevator that Anna Langford was in danger of losing a pregnancy. Nobody but Adam even knew that she was pregnant.

On Anna's floor, he stormed past the receptionist and down the hall, rushing inside her office. "I'm here. Let's go. The car is downstairs." His heart was still pounding—seeing Anna and the panic on her face turned everything into an even harsher reality. They could lose the baby.

Anna nodded, putting on her coat. He put his arm around her shoulders, ushering her out of the office. They didn't stop to say a thing to anyone. There was no time for explanations.

"I called Dr. Wright," she whispered as they waited for the elevator. "They're expecting us. She told us to come up to her office. Not the emergency room."

"Good. Okay. It's going to be okay." He had no business guaranteeing anything, but he had to believe it. They were so close to putting things back together. He rubbed her shoulder—anything to calm her, let her know that he was there for her.

Jacob got Anna down to the car and they were quickly whisked through the city, his driver breaking a few traffic laws while dodging taxis, cyclists and buses. Jacob put his arm around Anna's shoulder, pulling her close. She sank against him, turned into his chest, wrapped her arm around his waist. It was the only comfort he could take in that moment. They had each other. Whatever the future held for the two of them as a couple, or the three of them as a family, they would get through it. They had to.

When they arrived at the hospital, Jacob wasted no time getting Anna through the lobby and up to the sixth floor. The nurse was waiting for them and quickly showed them back to an exam room. Anna changed into a gown. Dr. Wright was in moments later.

"Ms. Langford. Mr. Lin. Before I say anything, I want to tell you both to take a deep breath." She motioned with both hands for them to calm down. "I know you're worried, but this isn't always a bad thing. Let's see what's going on."

Anna leaned back on the exam table and Jacob took her hand. She tilted her head, looking up at him as if he held all of the answers. He'd never felt so helpless in his entire life—the two things he cherished most in the world were right here, Anna and the baby—and there was very little he could do to truly keep them safe. How he longed to tell Anna that everything was going to be okay and to be certain of it.

Dr. Wright wheeled back on her rolling stool. "The good news is that your cervix is closed up tight. Let's listen to the heartbeat and make sure there's no sign of fetal distress."

Fetal distress. Those two words felt like a death sentence. The thought of their child in distress brought the most sickening feeling up from the depths of his gut. He hoped to hear that beautiful whoosh. *Please God, let us hear the whoosh.*

"Before we do this," Dr. Wright started. "I want you both to understand that this is very early days. If the baby is in trouble, there's not much we can do. I want to remind you that you're both so young. You have your entire lives ahead of you. Today doesn't have to be the end."

Jacob's gaze dropped to meet Anna's. Tears streamed down her cheeks. They welled in his as well. He couldn't even remember another time when he'd cried, but he couldn't have stopped it if he'd wanted to. His dream of a life with Anna could still happen, but it would be different if they lost the baby. Neither of them would ever be the same. He would still want her if the worst happened, but would she still want him? She'd worried that he might not be around for the long haul, but the reality was that the same could be wondered about her. Without this child binding them together, and with every mistake he'd made, would she want to walk away? He couldn't fathom how empty his life would be if that happened.

"We understand. Go ahead," Anna said to Dr. Wright.

Jacob nodded reluctantly. "Yes. Please. Go ahead."

The static and pops had a distinctly different tone to them this time—it was hope at odds with itself, a moment born of desperation while clinging to what you already have, not focused on what might be. He'd never piled so many wishes on a single moment before. Jacob looked right into Anna's eyes. If they were going to receive the worst of news, they would experience the pain of that instant together. She would not be alone. Anna clung to his hand, squeezing tight. Static buzzed. The speaker popped. Frantic crackles echoed.

And then the whoosh. *Whoosh whoosh whoosh.*

Anna's eyes sprang to life, quickly followed by her electric smile, jolting Jacob back to a state where he felt as if he could breathe again. Anna raised her head and looked down at her stomach. "The baby…"

"The heartbeat sounds perfect," Dr. Wright said.

"Thank God." The most profound relief Jacob had ever experienced threatened to knock him flat. He closed his eyes and his shoulders dropped from the solace of that perfect sound. He leaned down and cupped Anna's cheek then pressed a kiss to her forehead. His lips wanted to stay there, keep contact with her warm and wonderful-smelling skin.

Dr. Wright turned off the Doppler and sat back down on her stool. Jacob helped Anna back up to sitting.

"I'd like you on bed rest for the next twenty-four hours. Take it easy. It's very possible that this is just normal first trimester spotting and has nothing to do with any of your other issues."

"Normal?" Jacob asked.

"Yes, Mr. Lin. Normal. Possibly."

He'd never quite imagined his glee at hearing

that anything was normal, possibly, but there it was. He was ecstatic.

"You aren't out of the woods. There are never any guarantees. But I'd say that everything, for the moment, looks good. Go home. Relax. Together. Dad, no going into work. Stay with her and call me if anything goes wrong."

"You don't have to worry about that. I'm not going anywhere."

Eighteen

Jacob and Anna arrived at Jacob's apartment around one, after running to Anna's place to get her a few things. He insisted they would be more comfortable at his place. She had to agree, and it was also much closer to the doctor's office if they had to return. Although, as Dr. Wright had said, there wasn't much they could do but wait for the bleeding to stop. At least they would be doing it together.

Anna changed into pajama pants and a tank top, unfortunately finding a similar amount of blood when she used the bathroom.

"Well?" Jacob asked, sounding hopeful when she walked into his bedroom.

"Still spotting. But it's not any worse than before, so that's good." It felt as though she was shouldering the weight of the moment. Intellectually, she knew she had no control over the bleeding, but it was hard not to feel responsible. Perhaps that was the burden of being the messenger. It was okay. She'd take it.

"I don't want you to worry about it." He pulled back the comforter and patted the bed. "Your throne, m'lady."

She grinned and shook her head. He could be so silly if he wanted to be, but she knew for a fact that he wasn't like that with anyone else. He reserved his most unguarded moments for her. "Are those your PJs?"

"Of course. I'm not leaving you in this bed alone." He'd put on a T-shirt and basketball shorts. How she loved those glorious, lanky legs of his. "I figure we'll watch bad movies all afternoon. I haven't played hooky from work in well, forever, I guess."

"You know, I think I just want to talk for now.

Maybe take a nap." She climbed into bed and he did the same, on his side. This was indeed an odd setup, not really knowing the state of things between them. She knew how she felt—he'd obliterated her doubts about whether he'd fight for her. And he'd been right there with her at the doctor's office, holding her hand. He'd even cried with her, at that moment when they were waiting to hear if the baby was still okay. She knew then that her love for him had never gone away. There had just been other things in the way and she could see now that she'd put a few of those things there herself, or at least allowed them to remain.

"This wasn't exactly what I had envisioned when I was hoping to get you back into my bed," he said, punching his pillow a few times.

Anna laughed. "Right now, this is all the romance I can take." She watched as his expression became decidedly less jovial. "I didn't mean it like that, Jacob. Really. I didn't."

He nodded. "It's okay. I'm just trying to follow your cues. I'm waiting for the moment when you tell me that it's okay for me to love you again."

She rolled to her side and took his hand. Of course he was waiting for her. She'd been the guardian of every roadblock between them, making sure he knew the reasons they shouldn't be together. It felt as though the time had come for her to focus on the reasons they should. "Do you think you can? Love me again?"

"Anna, I never stopped loving you."

"Never? Not even for a minute? What about the day I barged into your office?"

He shook his head. "I still loved you that day. It simply hurt more then. That's all."

She thought of the awful things that had come out of her mouth that day—yes, he had done the unimaginable, but she shouldn't have been so determined to end things, no matter what. "I should have listened to you that day. I was hurt, but you were right about a few things. What you had done didn't change what was between us." She smiled when she noticed the way he was hanging on her every word. "In some ways, it was better that we fell in love in a vacuum, hiding our relationship from my family and the rest of the world. It was really the only way it could happen and be real. There was no outside influence."

"Just you and me, Anna. That's the way it should be. Just you and me." The smile that rolled across his face was so pure and unguarded, it took her breath away. "I love you more than you'll ever know. Forever." He leaned closer and brushed a strand of hair from her forehead. "I started to fall in love with you from that very first kiss, and my feelings have only gotten stronger."

His words floated around in her head—so beautiful, so lovely. She couldn't help but be swept up in the moment. "I'm sorry that being with me has been such a test."

He shrugged. "We tested each other. All couples do. We just got a lot of testing out of the way during those early days."

"In some ways, it's good. If we can survive all of that, we can definitely handle sleepless nights and diapers, the terrible twos and kindergarten."

"You make it sound so glamorous." He reached out and pressed his finger to the end of her nose.

"You know what I mean."

"But that's the baby, Anna. There's more than that ahead of us. If you want it. Do you want more?"

She suddenly found it difficult to breathe. Even if he was merely asking for them to spend more time together, the answer was yes, although she hoped for more. Much, much more. Even these few moments in bed together were enough to remind her that she didn't want anything other than him, at her side. "I do."

"Good, because I can't lose you again. You know that I'm a pragmatist. I deal with numbers all day long. I deal with absolutes. But the truth is that my love for you is an absolute."

The tears came. There was no stopping them. They rolled right down her cheeks. "That's the sweetest thing anyone has ever said to me."

"It's true. All true." Before she knew what was happening, he climbed out of bed and walked over to the dresser. When he turned, he held a blue Tiffany box in his hand.

Anna gasped. It was the most horrifically girly thing to do, but she couldn't help it. "Jacob. Are you?" She sat up in bed, wiping the tears from her face.

His eyes grew very serious. "Shhh. I only get one chance to get this right."

"I know. But I just want to make sure you're thinking about what's happening here. I might lose the baby. Will you still feel like this is the right thing to do if that happens?"

He perched on the edge of the bed. "Anna Langford, I love you with all of my heart and soul. If we lose the baby, that doesn't change my love for you. We will get through it together and we'll find a way to be stronger on the other side. In the end, all I want is you." He presented the box, which was dwarfed by the size of his hand. "If you'll do me the honor of becoming my wife, I promise to love you and put up with your family until my very last breath."

She smiled, staring down at everything he held in his hand—their future, happiness. This wasn't at all the way she'd ever dreamed this moment would transpire, but she wouldn't have traded it for anything. "I love you so much. I want nothing more than to have you as my husband."

He opened the box and plucked a gorgeous round solitaire in a platinum setting from the box. He slipped it onto her finger. It was a little big—in both band size and heft—but it was perfect.

She clasped her other hand over her mouth as she admired the ring and the way it sparkled. "It's absolutely beautiful. I couldn't ask for anything more. Literally. I'm not sure I could carry around a bigger diamond without some help."

He laughed quietly. "I swear it didn't look that big in the store."

"Of course it didn't. Your hands are huge."

"All I care about is seeing it on your hand. It couldn't make me any happier."

He leaned forward and kissed her, softly. It was the first time their lips had touched since the breakup, and it was as if she was being reborn. That gentle brush of a kiss told her just how much they were made for each other. If they weren't, they wouldn't have found a way. This was where she belonged, with him, on the other side of their troubles. Or at least a few of them.

"This would be the part where we tear off each

other's clothes and make love all night. Sorry about that," she said sheepishly.

"Don't worry. I can hold off for a few nights until the spotting stops. Then I'll make you mine." He cozied up next to her, wrapping his arm around her, making her feel as protected as she could've imagined. "In the meantime, we wait for what comes, and we go through it together."

She took a deep breath, fighting the tears that fought to take over again. She wouldn't cry—there had been too many tears in the last year, and now was a time to be happy. She would focus on Jacob, the ring. She would focus on the baby, on her hope that everything would turn out okay for once. "It's raining," she said, looking out the bedroom windows, with the glorious view of the city.

"Just like that night upstate."

"I guess it did rain that night, didn't it? I remember the puddles the next morning."

"It rained like crazy and you slept right through it."

"I take it you didn't?"

"Not a wink. I was too busy wondering how I was going to get past your brother to get to you."

"Well, you did it. Big props for that."

"Now we just need to hope he can take care of your other brother."

She turned to shush him. "Let's not talk about the bad. Let's just think about the good."

He smiled and pulled her closer, kissing the top of her head and raking his hands through her hair. "I have all the good I'll ever need right here in my arms."

With morning came the sun. After the steady deluge of rain all night, Jacob could only hope this was a good sign. He hadn't slept at all—consumed with a mix of gratitude for Anna's answer to his proposal and hope that today would bring good things.

Anna was asleep on her side, his arm draped over her. He loved having her back against his chest where he could feel her breaths—that steady, measured reminder that she was here again and wasn't leaving any time soon. They hadn't slept in the same bed in weeks. He'd remembered it as being wonderful, but it was even better with the promise that they would be together. Forever.

Anna stirred. As happy as he was to be able to talk to her, that feeling faded as he realized that she would soon get up and go to the bathroom and they would have news—good or bad.

"You're up," he said, pushing his hair from his face.

"I am," she answered, sleepily, shifting her weight and swinging her legs out from under the covers.

"Are you?" He nodded toward the bathroom.

"I am. Fingers crossed."

He sat up in bed. "Do you need me to come with you?"

She sighed and managed half of a smile. "I'm okay. I'll let you know what happens."

"Whatever happens, Anna. I'm here. Good or bad."

Anna tiptoed off to the bathroom. Jacob climbed out of bed, wondering when it would be okay to ask how things were going. Luckily, the flush of the toilet gave him his cue. "Well?"

he called from the other room, his heart threatening to pound its way out of his body.

"Nothing," she called back with an elated squeak. "No more spotting."

Jacob had never moved so fast, arriving at the bathroom door in a flash. "Really? Nothing?"

She nodded, going to the sink to wash her hands.

Thank God. He came up behind her, wrapped his arms around her waist. She was so stunning in the morning—fresh-faced, simply beautiful. The fact that she was carrying his child and had his ring on her finger made her that much more irresistible. He was the luckiest man in creation. "I am so glad."

"I know. Me, too." She looked down and pressed the palm of her hand to her belly. "Me, too."

"You know, you and I are going to make really cute babies," he said, kissing the top of her head. It was the truth—their children would be absolutely gorgeous.

Turning in his arms, she looked up at him. "Babies? Plural?"

"Of course. I want a whole pack of little Lins running all over the penthouse."

She coughed so loud she practically sputtered. "A pack of Lins?"

"Yes, Anna. I had to swallow my pride with your brother. I have to beat him at something. Surely you'll grant me that much."

"Sorry. I don't get your point. Beat him at what, exactly?"

"How ever many kids he and Melanie have, we'll just have one more."

"So this is about being competitive with my brother. That's going to get expensive, you know. What with college and keeping them all outfitted in tiny baby motorcycle jackets."

He laughed. Never had he imagined he could ever be so happy. "Anna, darling. You just leave that to me."

Epilogue

After everything over the last year, Anna had very much looked forward to dancing with her brother Adam at his wedding. She'd imagined the grand hotel ballroom, the legion of happy guests, stunning centerpieces of purple tulips and white irises picked out by Melanie, and the enormous wedding cake that likely took more than a week to create. She'd just never imagined that she'd be watching her other brother, Aiden, dancing with their mother at the same time.

"Aiden seems so happy to be back in the family fold," she said to Adam as he twirled her around the dance floor. He'd just finished his own dance with their mother, during which Evelyn Langford had cried her eyes out. Between having all three of her children in the same place for the first time in years and having her first grandchild on the way, Evelyn had made a point of telling them all how happy she was. There was much to be thankful for on this chilly January day, even the tears that flowed because of it.

"Aiden does seem happy, doesn't he?" Adam countered. "I still can't believe what a number Dad did on him, but I'm glad he was able to see past it. I know for a fact that it hasn't been easy for him."

Anna didn't even want to think about the things that had come to light about their father and his volatile relationship with Aiden—years of misunderstandings, Aiden being passed over in favor of Adam. She only wanted to focus on the good, especially today. "I think it helped a lot that you two talked everything out. He needed to feel like you weren't just toeing the family line because of your loyalty to Dad."

"I loved Dad as much as anyone, but we both know that he could be stubborn and narrow-minded. It doesn't mean he wasn't a good man. It just means that he made mistakes. We've all made mistakes. I've made a lifetime of them and I'm not even thirty-five."

Anna smiled. She wasn't about to rub it in, even though she very easily could have as pertained to Jacob. Adam and Jacob's friendship had rebounded nicely in the weeks since Jacob had dared to demand a truce. They weren't best friends, but they'd come to enjoy time together, and that was as much as she could've ever hoped for. "We all goof up, Adam. It takes happy days like today to remind us that sometimes we have to let those things go." That lesson had been no more important for her than when it had come to Jacob. The minute she put the past behind them, the future had opened up beautifully.

"Speaking of letting things go, why didn't one of us come up with the idea of running Lang-Tel together as co-CEOs? It's a brilliant move."

She smiled. This had been Jacob's idea, since they were already doing some restructuring in the company in order to bring Aiden on board as a Senior VP of Marketing. "Jacob made an excellent point. No two people are capable of accomplishing as much as we are when we aren't fighting." It wasn't exactly the arrangement Anna had expected. A few months ago, she would have said absolutely not, that she wanted the sole position for herself. But with her pregnancy progressing well, and with an early June due date, taking over as CEO would not leave her the time to be the kind of mom she wanted to be. Her career was important, but not so much that she wanted their child raised by a nanny. That existence had been so difficult for Jacob. She didn't care to repeat the pattern and understandably, neither did he.

"You don't need to worry about any fighting from me. I promise. The co-CEO thing means I can go back to working on my own projects, as well. It's really perfect for me."

"It's perfect for both of us," Anna added.

The song faded to its end and Jacob came up behind Adam with a wide grin on his face. "Hey, Langford. I don't want to be a jerk about it, but I'd like to dance with my bride-to-be."

Adam kissed Anna on the cheek. "Sounds like

somebody is tired of sharing you. I can't say I blame him." He clapped Jacob on the back. If anyone had said six months ago that this particular scene would be indicative of the new status quo, Anna never would've believed it. "I'll leave you two lovebirds to it. I have a date with my own bride." He excused himself and waved at Melanie, who was extricating herself from a dance with her uncle.

Jacob swept Anna into his arms, twirling her several times, making the eggplant purple bridesmaid's dress flutter around her. "Finally. I get you to myself."

Anna giggled, the swarm of wedding guests around them fading into the recesses as she became solely focused on Jacob. He really was her dream man. He really was perfect for her. And she couldn't have been any happier.

"We need to get in our time on the dance floor. Just a little more than a month until we're in this same spotlight." They did, in fact, need to clock a few hours of dancing, although their wedding would not be anywhere near as extravagant—fifty guests, at Jacob's house upstate. Neither one of them cared to deal with anything more elaborate. Jacob had actually said he was hoping for a blizzard so no one would be able to show up and he could keep Anna to himself for an entire week or more. She couldn't blame him. It sounded like the perfect plan.

He pulled her closer, his body heat enveloping her, or perhaps it was just his magnetism, the things about him that wouldn't allow her to stay away. He was especially difficult to resist in a tuxedo. "I can't believe you're going to be my wife. Honestly, I can't believe I'm going to be part of the Langford family. I'm having a hard time imagining what it's going to be like. Especially after spending six years in exile."

She reared her head back, looking deeply into his soulful eyes. "Things happen for a reason. I believe that. Maybe you and Adam will end up having an even stronger friendship one day. I certainly wasn't ready to run away with you and have a baby six years ago. So maybe this was for the best, as difficult as it was for you to go through."

He nodded, a slight smile crossing his face.

"I'd go through it all for you. Every last minute of it."

She smirked and shook her head. "You're sweet."

"Really I'm just angling to get you out of that bridesmaid's dress."

"You and me both. I can't wait to change. It's too tight on my belly." Anna wasn't showing much yet, but her tummy had pooched out a little. Jacob liked to lie in bed and talk to the tiny baby bump. Then he would get out his Doppler for listening to the heartbeat, which had arrived shortly after the spotting scare. He made quite the doting dad-to-be.

Jacob pulled her in tightly, moving her in time effortlessly to the music. "Are you happy?" he asked.

"What kind of question is that?" Anna whispered, leaning into him as she watched Adam and Melanie sway in the tiniest of circles, husband and wife. It wouldn't be long for Jacob and her. The thought warmed her from head to toe.

"It's a perfectly valid thing to ask, especially considering everything we've been through. I want to know that you're happy, Anna. It's the only thing I care about."

She looked up into his eyes, which shone down on her like sunshine on the first day of spring. She could get lost in those eyes for a lifetime and be deliriously giddy. "I don't think it's possible for me to be happier. Truly. Being with you is all I'll ever want."

"Good." He slowed their dance to the most imperceptible of movements, lowering his head and planting the sexiest, hottest kiss she could've imagined on her lips. It was slow and seductive, a subtle parting of lips and the most tasteful bit of tongue. It left her ready to pass out.

"Jacob. My family is watching," she said when she came up for air, making a mental note that they absolutely would need to continue this when they got home after the reception.

"I thought we agreed that your family had interfered in enough of our kisses."

"True, but it's still a wedding. We don't want to be *those* people, do we?"

He laughed and spun her around, then stopped and laid another steamy kiss on her, this time dipping her back in his arms. He left her breath-less, ready to surrender in a ballroom filled with hundreds of people. "Tell me to stop."

She smiled, caught in his eyes and the echo of the enticing rumble in his voice. "Jacob Lin, I never want you to stop."

* * * * *

MILLS & BOON®

Why shop at millsandboon.co.uk?

Each year, thousands of romance readers find their perfect read at millsandboon.co.uk. That's because we're passionate about bringing you the very best romantic fiction. Here are some of the advantages of shopping at www.millsandboon.co.uk:

* **Get new books first**—you'll be able to buy your favourite books one month before they hit the shops

* **Get exclusive discounts**—you'll also be able to buy our specially created monthly collections, with up to 50% off the RRP

* **Find your favourite authors**—latest news, interviews and new releases for all your favourite authors and series on our website, plus ideas for what to try next

* **Join in**—once you've bought your favourite books, don't forget to register with us to rate, review and join in the discussions

Visit **www.millsandboon.co.uk**
for all this and more today!